THE ENCHANTED ISLE

WHAT BECOMES A LEGEND MOST?

"OK Beautiful, you haven't answered me what I asked. You want a mink coat, is that it?"

"Well, who doesn't want a mink coat?"

"And you'd do what it takes to get it?"

"I'd like to hear more before answering that."

Because it came to me, if I had to sleep with him, or perhaps with the both of them, I wasn't so sure anymore that I'd do what it took, irregardless of what it was. But then he really surprised me. What I said was "What would it take to get it? What are you getting at?"

"Like robbing a bank, Beautiful."

THE ENCHANTED ISLE

James M. Cain

THE MYSTERIOUS PRESS • New York

MYSTERIOUS PRESS EDITION

Mysterious Press books are published in association
with Warner Books, Inc.
666 Fifth Avenue
New York, N.Y. 10103

A Warner Communications Company

Printed in the United States of America

Originally published in hardcover by Mysterious Press
First Mysterious Press Paperback Printing: July, 1986

10 9 8 7 6 5 4 3 2 1

1

So I went in the jewelry store, bought my ticket to Baltimore, and stepped out onto the street again, on my way to visit my father, to go to his arms and be loved. But if I actually meant to get on that bus, to leave my happy home (my more or less happy home), for good and all and forever, I didn't know then and don't know now. My father, my dreaming about him, my trying to be with him, is what I'm writing about, not so much that other thing, my helping out on the $120,000 holdup— so I don't look like such a jerk. So OK, maybe I was a jerk, but if so, I was a crazy jerk and not a silly one as the papers made me out. I am a girl, sixteen years old, five foot two, 36–24–35, 105 pounds, blond hair, blue eyes, with a so-so face and not-too-bad-figure—call it extra good. It's Mother's, and I could see what it was like when she walked around and when I looked at myself in the mirror without any clothes on, which I did often enough, perhaps oftener than I should. But if it's something special, that's not exactly my fault, and if it's partly what caused the trouble, that isn't my fault either. I'm putting it in just the same as the trouble, the whole trouble, has to go in too, or the rest of it makes no sense. And if it seems funny that I should tell it at all, instead of shutting up about it and letting it be forgotten, I can only say I'm not telling a thing that hasn't been already told, 'specially in the adoption papers, except they didn't tell it right, as I'm trying to do. So first off, about my name. It's Amanda Wilmer now, after the papers were taken on me week before last. Before that I was Amanda Vernick, as I'll explain. But everyone calls me Mandy, and now for what happened to me:

It really started before I was born, but I didn't know that at first, and so far as I was concerned it started three years ago, when Steve commenced beating me up. Steve, Steve Baker, was Mother's second husband, or at lease as I'd always thought, my stepfather, and at first I'd been nuts about him, his tricks that he'd play on me, his singing in the tub, and his jokes. I thought of him as my father and would climb all over him, wrestle with him, and race with him in the yard of the two-story house that we had, on a side street, back from the bank in Hyattsville, Maryland, which is eight miles from Washington, D.C. But then all of a sudden he changed and began beating me up—taking me over his knee, stripping my undies down, and smacking me with his hand. Well, when you're thirteen years old, that doesn't sit so good. The hurt meant nothing at all—him and ten like him couldn't have broke me, but him having the nerve, that bugged me. I screamed bloody murder and refused to say if I'd been running round, which was what he said I'd been doing. I hadn't been, though Amy Schultz had, a girl friend of mine that he knew, who did so much talking about it he thought I had too. And I might have, being human and perfectly normal, except the crumbs she ran with were no temptation to me. So I had nothing to tell, but when I wouldn't tell, he suspicioned me still more and beat me up still worse. And who thought it was nothing at all? Who said "Be nice to him!"—meaning giggle instead of scream—so he could "get going with me," and tension would be "relieved"? God rest her beautiful soul, but I have to say it of her, it was my darling mother. And if that seems funny to you, it seemed even funnier to me, as she knew and he knew and I knew why he did to me what I said before: spanking my more or less shapely backside, that he'd feel in between smacks and get a buzz off of.

So when the beatings started, she moved to her separate room, not sleeping with him anymore, and that matched up OK, except why wasn't she jealous of me? Why did she egg it on, as though throwing me at him? I couldn't figure it out, until one day I picked up the phone, the downstairs one in the hall, and upstairs she stopped talking quick and hung up. I knew then it was her that was stepping out and that that was the reason she had for not minding at all that Steve was messing with me. Then one day I staked her out—it was one of Steve's days in New York. He drove a truck, his own rig as he called it, part of a downtown fleet, Pan-Eastern Lines, Inc., and twice a week, Mondays and Thursdays, he hauled parcel post to New York, and wine off the boats coming back. So on a Monday I played hooky from school, and tucked away in the malt shop down on the boulevard till the laundry truck went up. Then I went and got in a cab and had it park across from the bank. And then sure enough, here she came, but instead of turning left for the bus stop as I expected, she turned right and crossed with the light, so she was just up the street from me. Then from behind my cab came a Caddy, a green Cadillac sedan, stopping between me and her. Then when it drove off she was gone. I told my driver to follow it, but when we got to the light it changed, and when it came green again the Caddy was out of sight and the driver refused to chase it. "I want to live, that's why—I just don't care to be dead."

"OK, take me home."

Twenty minutes later, though, I had what I wanted and more. She had taken the laundry in, but it was still in the lower hall and, of course, I put it away. However, I missed a gingham dress, and thinking it might have got in with her things, I looked in her bureau drawers. And sure enough it was, with the aprons she had sent out. But under the pillow slips, tucked away nice and neat, was a letter. I certainly wouldn't have opened it if it hadn't been for the address, which was to her, "Care General Delivery, Hyattsville, Md." That seemed very peculiar, and I decided to have a look. Inside was a newspaper piece, a clip from the *Baltimore Sun*, about a Benjamin Wilmer, the story of his life, also a picture of him, quite a good-looking guy. It seemed he'd been born in Baltimore, and gone to City College, before coming into some land that his father had had when he died, at Rocky Ridge in Frederick County, known as "Wilmer's Folly" from its being all rock and scrub woods, not worth the taxes it paid. But it had a stream running through it, with riparian rights attached, whatever they were, and when he had it analyzed, it was right for fermenting grain. So he dammed it, made a lake, put in power, and started a bonded distillery. Now it had all paid off, so he was a leading citizen, one of Frederick County's "more eligible bachelors." Enclosing the clip was a note, giving her his love, and saying the Caddy was ordered, in green to blend with her hair. Her hair is dark red, and she dotes on bottle-green.

So that named the guy, but it didn't clear anything up. Because if he was such an eligible bachelor, and if he had dough for a Caddy to blend with her hair, why wasn't he having it done? Shipping her out to Reno, melting the thing with Steve, and marrying her himself? Why wasn't she making him do it? It wasn't as though she was bashful. Outside she was soft and pretty and meek, like butter wouldn't melt in her mouth. But inside she wasn't meek and could melt butter fast. She could crack the whip, and it seemed funny she hadn't. And on top of that there was Steve. If I knew she was playing around, he knew she was playing around, and why was he letting her do it? Why hadn't he thrown her out? The more I thought about it, I was the answer both ways— with her, that she couldn't get married until she was rid of me, which meant throwing me at Steve. And with him, that he'd never make a move, to throw her out or anything, if he thought it meant losing me. So there I was in the middle, and I commenced getting the creeps. And it may not sound like much, but I'd have died before going to Steve—*that* way I'm talking about. And the worst of it was I was fifteen years old and had no one on this earth, not one human being, to take up for me. If you hear of a child acting crazy, you ask about that first of all—if she has a father that kicks her around and a mother that lets him do it. With no one to take up for her, she can go haywire fast. It's the first thing you want to find out, before sending her to reform school. Maybe she's not the one to reform.

So in the dark I would lie there, and then I knew I had to leave home. Where I would go I didn't know, except it seemed to boil down to a life of shame, which had a mink coat attached, at lease so I'd heard; or a convent, which had a nun habit. We were Episcopal, but they have Episcopal nunneries too, and I'd heard they'd take you in. Either way I'd get even, parade in front of Mother and Steve in the mink coat or nun habit, whichever, and say, "You made me what I am today, I hope you're satisfied." And then it came to me, and came to me night after night: I didn't have to do that, go for the shame or the convent, neither of which really appealed to me, as I did have someone out there to take up for me. That was my father, my real father I'm talking about, at lease as I thought he was then—that I'd never heard from, at Christmas or Valentine's or even on my birthday. But who said he knew where I was? Could be that Mother hadn't told him, as they'd broken up when I was born and she never spoke of him. But I began imagining him, how good-looking he was, and how we'd live, us two, on a desert isle we'd swim to when our plane was wrecked at sea, and eat clams and drink coconut milk. I got so I knew every tree, every bunch of grass, every stretch of sand on that island I had with him. Then I knew I was going to him, and once more I played hooky from school.

It was another Monday morning, early in June, a month ago, and once more Steve had driven in to the District to start his trip to New York. Once more I sat in the malt shop, once more Mother appeared, once more the Caddy stopped, once more it started off and she wasn't there anymore. I went back to the house and packed, taking my time about it. I put my things in my zipper bag, the one I'd had at the beach—my dresses, some shorts, socks and other stuff, and one extra pair of shoes, but I put some loafers back as they took up too much room. I put on a blue mini dress. I put on a black straw hat, one I'd worn to church but OK, I thought, for travel. I counted my money, the thirty I'd made from odd jobs, the sixteen for baby-sitting, and the twenty-eight I had left over from delivering papers. I wrote Mother a note, pretty mean I guess, saying I was fed up but telling her good-bye and Steve good-bye. I left it on the hall table, picked up my bag and coat, walked down to the jewelry store, and, like I said, bought my bus ticket to Baltimore. Then I went out on the street again, but if I tell the truth, in my secret heart I didn't know what I meant to do—get on the bus and go through with it, or walk on back to the house, tear up my note, and go on as I had been going.

But on the bench, when I got to it, was a boy.

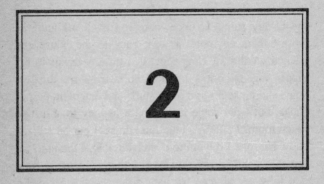

2

When he saw me he got up and took my bag and coat. He was medium height and kind of good-looking, except for the slant of his face, off to one side, with dark hair, black eyes, and sideburns. He had on gray slacks and a zipper jacket and looked around nineteen, three years older than I was. But when he sat down again, it wasn't beside the bag and coat, but between me and them, kind of close, which was OK with me, except he was kind of rank from not having had a bath. I didn't mind too much, but didn't like it much either. However, no use magnifying small things, so when he said "Hiya," I did, and we took it from there. He said what nice weather we were having, and I said yeah, it sure was. He said it was generally balmy in June, and I said there was that about it. We went along like that a few minutes, and then he asked if I was taking the bus. I said, "Yeah," and then right away took it back, because, like I said, I wasn't sure yet, down deep inside me, if I was taking that bus or not. I stammered, "I mean, I'm thinking about it. I . . . have my ticket bought, but I haven't decided yet." But then at last, for no good reason at all, except he was looking at me, except he *kept* looking at me, like I must be some kind of a kook, I did make up my mind— I knew I was taking that bus. I said, "Yeah, I've pretty well made up my mind. I guess I'm taking it, yeah." And then: "I am! You can bet your sweet life on that!" And then, blurting it out, still for the same reason of how he was looking at me: "I'm leaving home if you have to know! I'm going to Baltimore! I'm going to find my father—my real father I'm talking about, not this other one, the one that beat me up!"

". . . The one that *what*?"

"I'm sorry. I shouldn't unload on you."

"Well, hey! It's what a friend is for, isn't it?"

"I could use one all right."

He patted my hand, and we sat for some little time. Then: "I'm leaving home too, and I'm bound for Baltimore too. But I'm different from you—I'm not leaving, I was put. Out, I mean, like Bill Bailey, except without any fine-tooth comb till I bought myself one." He took a comb from his pocket and waved it around at me. Then he went on, "Without *anything*, if you can believe it. Some friends took me in, but this morning *they* put me out. Stuff was missing from the pantry, and they said I took it and sold it. I said I hadn't. I offered to prove I hadn't, but would they let me? Would they believe what I said? Why is it my father, my mother, my friends, everyone except maybe my sister, got to believe somebody else, not me? Why can't they *ever* believe me?"

"I've been through that, plenty."

"But why? Will you tell me?"

"With that stepfather of mine I know why—I hope to tell you I do. I'd be ashamed to say. I'd be ashamed even to breathe it."

". . . When does your bus come through?"

"Twenty after. But I thought it was your bus too."

"I wish it was. I'd love to travel with you, and Baltimore's where I'm bound. The thing of it is I'm flat. I told you how they put me out—without a comb, without a brush, without a dime, and without one word being said about the two hundred they owe me, that they're holding for me, that they're *supposed* to be holding for me, that by rights ought to be mine. . . . How much money you got?"

". . . Little over seventy-four dollars."

"Look, if you could lend me two dollars, then I could buy me a ticket and keep you company on this trip."

"OK."

"Thanks. You're swell. What's your name?"

"Mandy—Mandy Vernick. It's really Amanda, but Mandy's what they call me. What's yours?"

"Rick. Rick Davis."

"Rick? That's for Richard?"

"Yeah, sure."

"I like it better than Dick."

By then I had out my billfold to give him the money. He said, "Make it five—then I can hold my head up."

So I made it five.

He went and bought a ticket, and then our bus came along, "three-twenty, right on time," as he said, taking a flash at my watch. It was half full, but the back seat was empty and we took it, me sitting next to the window, him putting my bag and coat topside, in the rack over our heads. We passed a meadow off to one side, with a plane taxiing on it, a little yellow plane, and he said, "The College Park Flying Field—oldest one in the world. Did you know that, Mandy?"

"I never even heard of it."

"Well, it is."

That was the whole conversation for at lease half the trip. The bus was a local, stopping every three or four miles, but we held hands and didn't mind. Then, though, I started talking, half to myself, and it all commenced coming out, about Steve, the real reason he had for spanking me, and even about Mother, who I shouldn't have mentioned at all but had to; I just couldn't help it. And yet I mightn't have if it hadn't been for him, listening so sympathetic. Seems funny, the way he treated me later, that I didn't catch on at the time the kind of a guy he was. But I didn't and went on and on, at last even telling about my father and how I would call him up soon as I got into the bus station in Baltimore. But then for the first time, 'stead of being so sympathetic, he shook his head no. "What's the matter, Rick? I say something out of line?"

"Mandy, it's none of my business—tell me shut my big mouth and I shut it. But that don't sound good to me; it don't sound good at all."

"How do you mean it don't sound good?"

"Well? Suppose he's not home. What then?"

"I can wait, can't I? And call again?"

"Suppose he's out of town?"

". . . I hadn't thought of that."

"Suppose he married after the bust-up? The one he had with your mother? Suppose his wife answers?"

". . . I can ask to speak to him, can't I?"

"Suppose she asks who's calling?"

"Well? Can't I say?"

"And she says, 'Oh my, I didn't realize! Oh my, will you hold, Miss Vernick? Oh my, he speaks of you often! Oh my, he'll be so excited!' In the pig's right eye she will."

"You mean she wouldn't like it?"

"Well, would you?"

". . . OK, what am I going to do?"

"Hold everything, let me think."

So he thought, and then: "One thing you should do, Mandy, is give it the old switcheroo, so 'stead of you leading to him, he'll be leading to you. I mean, forget that pitch, that you call him and then he'll ask you there— to his house, or wherever it is that he lives. Fix it that he comes to you—it'll make all the difference, all the difference in the world. Meaning you must have a place to stay, a place you can ask him to, so he comes to see *you*!"

"How do you mean, a place?"

"Well, like an apartment."

"I see, I see."

"Then *you* invite *him*, like a lady does."

"OK. But I can't get a place tonight."

"It's what's been bothering me, Mandy."

"I'll have to go to a motel."

"*That*'s what's been bothering me. You can't."

"Why can't I?"

"They won't take you in, that's why. A young girl? Alone? Wants a single and bath? For what purpose, Mandy? For all they know, you could be using that room for business of a very peculiar kind."

"Oh."

"There's plenty of *that* going on."

"Well, what *am* I going to do?"

"I've been figuring on it, and I'm your friend, no? And what's a friend for? We could go to the motel together."

". . . You mean, as Mr. and Mrs.?"

"Well, who's going to know the difference?"

"I'd have to think about that."

Then I told him, "OK."

"I already said, you're swell."

"Rick, what name are we going to use?"

"Well, there's a Baby Ruth sign—why not John P. Ruth and wife?"

"Better make it Richard P. Ruth—I might call you Rick by mistake, tip them off without meaning to."

"Richard P. Ruth is good. Mrs. Ruth, hiya?"

"I'm fine, Mr. Ruth—how's your own self?"

We both laughed and squeezed hands, and then I said, "Rick, there's a motel—a little one, maybe not so expensive as the others. And we're already in Baltimore. I've been here before and can tell by the brick houses with white doorsteps."

"That motel was put there for us. OK."

He got my bag and coat down, and at the next stop, which was in the same block as the motel, we got off.

3

At the motel the room was small and beat-up, but at lease it had twin beds, a bathroom with clean towels in it, and a bureau with big-enough drawers. But he hardly seemed to see it or notice what it was like, because all during the time I was putting my things away, and he was putting *his* things away—his razor, toothbrush, and comb, which seemed to be all he had—he was crabbing and crabbing and crabbing about what happened down at the desk. There, soon as he'd signed the card and asked for a double with bath, the woman said, "Second floor front. That'll be eight dollars, please." I was kind of surprised, as there was my luggage beside me, my zipper bag that I had, but paid with a ten-dollar bill, and when she gave me my change and key, I started upstairs. Rick followed along with the bag, but when we got to the room he burst out, "How does she get that way? Making us pay in advance? We look like bums or something?" I said it was more of the same, what he had mentioned before: "We're kids and no one believes us, that we'd pay for our room or *anything*. Always, we get the short end of the stick."

For me that covered it, but he went on and on, taking the one chair that we had, while I sat on one of the beds, and he kept going on, even while we ate dinner, which we did around six o'clock, at a coffee pot up the street, an all-night joint that the woman directed us to. We both had the roast beef sandwich and buttermilk, and pie a la mode for dessert. And on the eight dollars, I would like to have given it a rest, but he kept on about it—so even the counterman threw me a wink—about the dirty tricks being played on him by everyone, especially by his father. He'd go into a long, mixed-up story that didn't make any sense, like about the tires that had been hid in the family garage, then found there by the police, and then begin asking questions that didn't have any answers: "Could I know that bunch would steal those tires, then stash them in our garage? Would he believe me, that I didn't know they were there? Why would he pay for that loot? To save me, as he said? From having to go to Patuxent? Or to make me look like a bum?" Then, when I'd kind of lost track, he'd switch off to another mixed-up thing, about slinging sodas the previous summer. Then: "And that drugstore, reporting me on my cash to him, that I was short. Would he believe I wasn't? Would he make them come up with their slips, so I could prove I was clean? Oh, no, he had to pay, for the same noble reason—to keep me from doing time." And next, the bitterest squawk of all, was about some girl who lived next door to him and gave him $7.50 she had made selling

Girl Scout cookies door-to-door to keep for her until Monday, so she wouldn't spend it Saturday night. And: "When I gave it back to her, she said it was seventeen-fifty, that I'd nicked her out of a tenspot that was part of the money. I hadn't. I know what she gave me, don't I? But would my father believe what I said? I give you one guess if he would. Once more he paid, but this time he said was the last—that's when he put me out."

And that's when I wanted to tell him, "Cool it, enough is enough." But then I thought, "Wait a minute, Mandy! Who talked whose ear off today coming in on the bus? And who listened real nice? Took your side and did the best he knew how to help you out of your spot? He did, that's who. So fix up your face and keep still. Maybe he does have a squawk. The lease you can do is listen." So I did, saying, "Oh my, I can hardly believe it" and "That was really awful" and "Your father would do that to *you*?" All while we were finishing dinner I talked like that, and during the walk we took afterward. It seemed funny later, when I drove the getaway car after we held up the bank, that those places I had to know to do my part right I'd already noticed real close on the walk I took that night: the chopper-blade factory, a two-story concrete building with black marble framing the entrance and THE COLYPTE CORPORATION in brass letters over the door and a chopper blade over that; the branch bank of the Chesapeake Banking and Trust Company, a block and a half beyond the stoplight, on the cross-street in between; and the phone booth on the cross-street, a half block up from the bank, where it crossed my mind for a moment that I could call Mother and ease her mind, but what crossed my mind next was: I didn't want to.

* * *

It was still not yet eight o'clock when we got back to the motel, though with daylight saving time it was broad daylight. But we bought two *Evening Suns* and after watching TV a few minutes went on up to the room. Then for the first time Rick made a pass: "Well, what do you say, Mandy? We having a roll in the hay?"

"Well? It's what hay is for, isn't it?"

We both laughed and that's all there was to it—but telling the truth about it, I wasn't too excited one way or the other. And I added on real quick, "I tell you one thing, though: you're taking a bath first, Rick. You ought to be ashamed of yourself, to smell the way you do. You heard what I said: you smell. We could almost say S-T-I-N-K."

"Well, look at the life I've been leading."

"And you could dunk some of what you're wearing. You wash those things out good, then hang them up over the tub to drip-dry on that shower-curtain rail."

"OK, OK, OK."

"Take one of my nighties to sleep in."

I got it for him. "What's the matter with skin?"

"I'm a nice girl. Put something on."

But he'd hardly closed the bathroom door when I dropped him out of my mind. Because I thought: why must I wait? Wait till I have an apartment before calling my father? I could do it right now. I could do it here from this room. I don't have to give him that name, the one Rick wrote on the register. I could give him my real name, his name of course, and then meet him downstairs in the lobby—be waiting for him there when he comes. Then I could make a fresh start, forget this thing with

Rick and the roll in the hay he expects. It's still early evening, exactly the right time, so I got the phone book from the night table, took it to the window, and looked, and sure enough he was in it, Edward Vernick, at an address on West Lombard Street. I called the desk and gave the woman the number, then sat on the bed, patted myself on the heart, and tried to make it calm down. But all it did was pound. After some rings a woman answered. I said, "Mr. Vernick, please."

"Who's calling?"

". . . He doesn't know me, Ma'am."

"I have to say who it is."

". . . Tell him Mandy."

". . . Tell him—*who*?"

"He'll know if you tell him. Mandy."

All that got was a long silence, but then a man came on the line. "Edward Vernick talking. Who is this, please?"

"Mr. Vernick, it's Mandy."

"I'm sorry, the name means nothing to me."

"I'm your daughter, Mr. Vernick. Mandy."

It was so long before he answered that I thought the connection was broken and asked him if he was there. At last he said, "Yes, I'm here, but I don't *have* any daughter and don't know *anyone* named Mandy. You're under a misapprehension, or someone's been telling you falsehoods. But whatever the reason is, don't call me again, and don't come to this house. You'll not be let in if you do. Do you hear me?"

"Yes, sir, I do."

"And don't expect any money."

". . . Money? Is that what you said, *money*?"

"I said don't ask it. You'll not get it."

"Well, who's asking money of you? Who wants money of you? Who *needs* money of you? How did money get in it?"

"Whether you ask it or want it or need it, you're not going to get it. Am I making myself clear?"

"You make yourself any clearer I can see right through to your backbone how much like a snake it looks."

"Is there anything else?"

"I hope to tell you there's not."

"Then I bid you good-bye."

Next off Rick was there in my nightie, which was so short on him it was funny, a foolish look on his face, and I was in the chair, with no idea how I got there. I'd been on the bed with the phone and didn't remember moving or anything. All I knew was I was gooped from that call, like I'd been hit by a truck. I mean I didn't feel anything except queer between the eyes. And when he began making comical cracks, about me not being undressed, and then trying to drag me to bed, I wasn't with it at all. I just sat there, shaking him off and not saying anything. I came out of it little by little, but when I did, brother, did I burn. I started to burn and started to talk, saying what I thought of that Vernick. And when Rick finally got it, put it together from what I was saying, what had been said on the phone, he joined in and helped out. "But, Mandy, who told you so from the start? That that idea was a louse?"

"You did, I give you credit."

"And who told you the guy was no good? Because he walked out on your mother? Who let you sit there year after year, in Hyattsville, without once calling you up or even sending a card?"

"You did, I have to say you did."

"That crummy son of a bitch."

"It's what I want to call him."

"Then call him, you're entitled."

"That crummy son of a bitch."

"Feel better now?"

"Little bit. Thanks."

"Then come on to bed—I'll make you feel well all the way. My but you're pretty, Mandy. Your legs are out of this world."

". . . Rick, I couldn't."

"Why not?"

"I feel sick, that's why."

"But I got the medicine for it."

"Please, don't ask it, Rick. I'm sorry, I meant to, just now when we talked about it, and even on the bus it's what I thought we would do. But I've been hit, something has happened to me, and I can't. It's bugging me, what he said, and until I do something about it, it'll keep on bugging me."

"Yeah, like I said, do it with me."

"That's not what I'm talking about."

"What are you talking about?"

". . . Mink coat."

Because that was it, I knew a nun habit wouldn't do for what I was dreaming about: that I'd taxi to Lombard Street, parade myself up and down in front of his door in that coat, and holler, "Does this look like I need your money? Does your wife have one, Mr. Vernick? Are you sure it's *me* that needs dough?" And more of the same in my mind, which, of course, I could not say to Rick. So what I did, I repeated, "Mink coat," sounding more or less off.

"What in the hell are you talking about? Mandy, maybe I'm dumb, but between this Vernick and mink coats, I just don't see the connection."

"There *is* one, at lease for me."

"Well, the hay might cool you off."

"Rick, I told you forget it."

"Oh, that's all, it's nothing, forget it."

"OK then, go ahead and spoil everything."

"*Me* spoil it? Mandy, you're the one."

There was quite a lot more, as he had his mind on one thing, and he even yanked me by the arm, trying to get me to bed. But when a girl don't want to be yanked, she don't yank so easy, and so I didn't move. At last he went to bed, and by what was left of the twilight I opened the *Evening Sun*. He said, "Quit rattling the paper, will you? If you're not going to do anything, at least you could let me sleep."

"Have to look in the want ads, find me a job."

"Job? Job, did you say?"

"That's right, J-O-B, job."

"Well, for Christ's sake, Mandy! First it's a mink coat, now it's a job! What's it going to be next?"

"Oh, one thing can lead to another."

"What thing? Leading to which other?"

"Well, I don't know yet, but I have to eat and have to have an apartment—even you said that." And I didn't say it, but thought: the apartment can lead to the shame and the shame can lead to the mink coat. And if you think about it, well, shame was right there in the bed, if that's all I was thinking about. It meant nothing to me at that time, as he couldn't give me a coat, a mink coat I'm talking about. He sat up in the bed and stared, then said, "Mandy, I think you're nuts."

"Well, maybe two of us do."

"Will you come to bed?"

"Soon as I look through the paper."

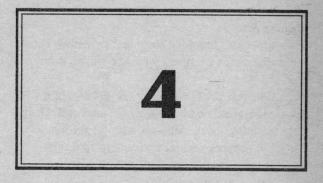

4

In the morning he was still sleeping when I got up, and I expected to do a sneak, leaving a note for him while I went out and had breakfast and took the bus for the job I'd picked out. It said "Waitresses Wanted," in a place called Gardenville, which I looked up on the Yellow Pages map and found out was on Bel Air Road, the other side of town. It meant a ride to the bus terminal, to start a new trip from there, and as "Apply Before 10 A.M." was what it said in the ad, I had to start pretty early if I was to get there in time. So by 6:30 I was up. I took his things from the bathroom, where they were hanging over the tub, spread them out on the chair, then went in and bathed and put on my clothes, the same ones as the day before. But when I came out he was standing in front of the bureau, all dressed, combing his hair, and smelling of my cologne. "What you doing, Mandy? Taking a powder on me?"

"Thought I'd let you sleep is all."

"What is this job you're going for?"

I told him. "And where does the mink coat come in? You think you can buy one of them with the tips a waitress gets?"

"I told you, one thing could lead to another. I could meet someone as a waitress who'd be willing to buy me one."

"If he was able, you mean. I never heard of a waitress meeting someone who bought her a mink coat. There's only one thing about waitresses: they all got sore feet."

"But not sore behinds from sitting on them."

"Is that a crack?"

"Take it any way you like."

By then I was packed, and I suppose he was, with his razor, comb, and toothbrush in his pocket where he carried them. So I led the way downstairs, carrying my bag and coat. I was about to pay for my call, the one I'd made from the room, but he pulled me back and whispered, "You want to get me checked out? So long as that call's outstanding, we're in until six o'clock and I still have a place to come."

"I'm sorry, I didn't get all the fine points."

But like before, he entertained me at breakfast by crabbing, and it was a different counterman, but he threw me a wink too. And on top of the crabbing, he got off these words of wisdom: "Mandy, it makes no sense, none of it does. Come on back to the motel so we can talk things over."

"I'm sorry, it makes sense to me. If it's the last thing I do on this earth, I mean to get me a mink coat."

"I wouldn't mind buying you one."

That was a guy at one of the tables, a big, thick-chested guy, sitting with three other guys, all from Co-lypte it seemed, and having breakfast here at the coffee pot after a night on the graveyard shift as they called it from time to time. I said, "Keep on talking, Big Boy. I mean to have me one, and any reasonable offer will get a receptive hearing. Do you have the price of one?"

"How about a package deal?" one of the other guys asked. "Suppose we all chipped in and kind of took turns on you, like in a secretary pool?"

"Or in a hippie commune?"

"Yeah, but we'd all take a bath."

"Keep talking, you interest me. Like I said, I'm out for a mink coat and will do what it takes to get one. But the first thing it takes is cash, and that I'll have to see before we sign any papers."

"Baby, do we go for you!"

And more of the same, all sociable, all with laughing mixed in. If I meant it I can't really say, though I must say I sounded quite wild. However, that was as far as it got, and I paid for the bacon and eggs, Rick's as well as mine, left a dollar tip, picked up my bag, and started down to the bus stop, buttoning my coat as I went. So, of course, here came Rick. I walked to the bench and sat down, and lo and behold, so did he. I asked, "You taking the bus too?"

"Well, OK, if you want me."

"It's not a question of wanting. It just wouldn't help, that's all, you sitting around while I ask for that job."

"Then you *don't* want me?"

"I can't have you, Rick."

"You coming back here?"

"Well, this job is on the other side of town, and I would think a nearer place would be indicated. An apartment, like you said."

"Then, it's good-bye?"

"Not necessarily. I can write you where I am."

"Write me? What address you going to use?"

"Why, 'Care General Delivery, Baltimore, Maryland.'"

"Are you being funny or what?"

"Then, OK, Rick, you say what address."

"How do I know where I'm going to be?"

"Well, you don't have to start acting snotty."

What he was really leading to, as I knew, was to hit me for more money, and I wanted to give him some, maybe another five, maybe even a ten. But I was afraid if I took my billfold out, he'd grab it off me and run, and what I would do then I didn't really know. What I *could* do, I mean. Because supposing I called a cop and he said the money was his, how could I prove it wasn't? He'd said stuff like that before, from those stories he'd told me at dinner. And supposing the cop believed me instead of him, what would he do then? Hold me and call Mother? Or maybe Mr. Vernick, as his name was in the phone book? That would be nice, wouldn't it? So I kept my handbag under my arm, the arm away from him, meaning to scream and bite if he wrestled me for it. So things were getting rugged, when all of a sudden two guys were there, both in jackets and slacks, and both with a strange look. I mean, 'stead of shirts in wash colors that most men wear, their shirts were dark blue or maybe black, with light ties, kind of sporty. One was kind of good-looking, around twenty-five, medium size, but nicely set up. The other, perhaps a year or two older, had a long lantern jaw, kind of blue, but fresh-shaved. It was the good-looking guy who spoke: "Hiya, Beautiful."

". . . Well. . . . Hiya."

"So you want a mink coat, is that it?"

"Who wants to know?"

Rick snarled it, though who gave him the right I don't know, as I didn't ask him to. And he jumped up, all ready to make himself objectionable. But the guy did not get upset. He said, "I do. I'm kind of curious about her. And you don't mind, do you?" So with that he opened his coat, and out from under his arm was peeping the butt of a gun.

". . . No, I don't mind. OK."

"OK, what?"

"OK, sir."

"I thought that's what you meant. Sit down."

Rick sat down again, and I told him, "These gentlemen want something, Rick, that has something to do with my coat, and I'll thank you to cool it now and let them say what's on their mind."

"OK, Mandy."

"We're not using names today."

That was still the good-looking guy, who seemed to do most of the talking. He went on, "Call me Pal. My friend here, my sidekick, call him Bud. The young lady already has answered to Beautiful, and you can be Chuck. Are we all straightened out on that?"

Rick and I both said we were, and he pumped at me some more. "OK, Beautiful, you haven't answered me what I asked. You want a mink coat, is that it?"

"You seem to know. How?"

"It's what you said, there in the beanery."

"Oh, you were in there too?"

"In the booth, having breakfast, yeah."

"Well, who doesn't want a mink coat?"

"And you'd do what it takes to get it?"

"I'd like to hear more before answering that."

Because it came to me, if I had to sleep with him, or perhaps with the both of them, I wasn't so sure anymore that I'd do what it took, irregardless of what it was. But then he really surprised me. What I said was "What would it take to get it? What are you getting at?"

"Like robbing a bank, Beautiful."

". . . Are you being funny?"

"Is that funny to you?"

"Well, I guess not. Not really."

"It's not funny to me either. OK, 'stead of all that beating and batting and banging around the bush, putting you in a pool, or whatever their idea was back in the greasy spoon, I got a proposition for you that'll get you a mink coat today, a coat you can wear tonight, swing if that's what you like in some club. And pretty as you are, you'll be something to see. So what do you say? Will you do what it takes or not?"

"I say maybe, but I have to know more about it."

"That answer pleases me."

He turned to his friend, Bud, who nodded and said, "We don't want no silly Jane that'll jump off the roof if you tell her to. If she wants to hear more, it proves she's got some sense."

"Beautiful, what do you want to know?"

"In the first place, on something like this it takes

people who know what they're doing, so why would you want me, who knows nothing about it at all? Or do you want both of us? Or what?"

". . . You done?"

"Well, that's what I want to know *first*."

"OK, we did have a mob, exactly the right-size mob, because the way we work it takes four. We don't go in, shove a note under the window, and take what the girl hands out. We clean the joint out, and to do it that way takes four: one outside at the wheel of the getaway car; and three in the bank, two of us holding guns, the other holding the basket while the girl throws money in it. But the mob we did have we don't have, not anymore we don't. Because two boys who've been helping us out, two brothers who know their stuff, when we went to wake them this morning, one was stoned on horse, and the other wouldn't leave him. So that puts us in the hole. But the job, if it's going to be done, has to be pulled today. Today's when the money is there, the extra payroll cash, and we dare not put it off, as maybe the word gets around, maybe the air smells funny, maybe something tells the cashier and he plays his hunch. From being in the hole we'd be in the soup, which we don't really enjoy. Make a long story short, if today is the day, we need someone, and you fell into our lap—on account of you wanting that mink coat. Now, does that clear it up for you?"

"Well . . . yeah. I guess so. A little."

"Chuck?"

". . . There's just one thing: so she wants a mink coat and that's why you picked us out. But why would you trust us on something like this? How do you know

I won't call the cops? Phone from the motel and tell them there's a couple of guys outside fixing to rob a bank."

"OK, go ahead and call."

". . . You mean now?"

"Sure. By the way, what you going to tell them?"

"Like I said, that you're fixing to rob a bank."

"Which bank?"

"Well, I don't know, you haven't said."

"If you don't know which bank, you've got nothing to tell. It's not against the law, fixing to rob a bank, if you don't know which bank it is, so they can set up their stakeout. They can't take me in for fixing. But they can take *you* in, and will."

". . . Take *me* in? For what?"

"Protective custody it's called."

"Protective? From what?"

"From having happen to you what generally happens to guys who rat."

"Now, I've got it. OK . . . sir."

"I'm glad you have. Do you drive?"

"Yes, sir."

"Beautiful?"

"I do, of course. But there's something I have to do—go to the motel and pay for my call." I explained about it and said, "I want to wind it up, so it's not on their books and not on their mind. It's a little thing, but I don't want it to dangle."

He stood staring at me, and I knew what was in his mind: that I wouldn't have to phone the cops, just tell the woman to do it, and then come back real quick with a grin on my face and stall till the squad car came. At last he said, "OK, I'll go with you."

"*No!*"

That was Bud, coming to life like he was hit with a whip and proving at last that he was more than a stooge. He lit into Pal but rough: "You want to throw it away, the one edge they give us, spite of their both being punks? That nobody's seen them with us, to idemnify? You go in with her, every goddam jerk in the motel can crucify you in court. It makes sense, what she says. I say let her go."

"OK, Beautiful. Go."

So I walked up to the motel, went in, and paid. When I came back, Bud said, "Let me look at you, kid."

"Right in the eye, Mr. Bud. You see something shifty?"

"OK."

"I want that coat."

"I said OK."

Bud asked, "Are we set?"

"There's just one thing, sir."

That was Rick. Pal said, "OK, Chuck, what is it?"

"This money, this dough we're supposed to get, how's it going to be split, Mr. Pal?"

". . . Why, four ways, of course."

"And when?"

"Soon as we switch cars. On a thing like this we use two to throw off whatever's on our tail. Once in the second car, we can stop and make the split—put Beautiful's share, and yours, in your bag, our share in our bag, which we have in the first car. Then we set you two down, you flag a cab and go with Beautiful, help her pick out the coat. You still don't know us, who we are, to tell any tales, and likewise we don't know you. Fair enough?"

"I guess so. OK, sir."

"Beautiful?"

"I already said. *I'm* in."

"Let's go."

5

He picked up my bag and led to the parking lot, the one in back of the coffee pot. He took keys from his pocket, unlocked a black sedan, then handed the key ring to Rick, telling him, "O.K., Chuck, let's see how you handle a car." But Bud cut in: "Not him, the girl. When we wind up the heist I want this car to *be* there." So Pal took the ring from Rick and gave it to me, first picking out the key I would want, and told me, "Get in there, take it away." So I did, slipping the key in the ignition and starting the motor, then lifting the door locks so he and Rick and Bud could get in on the other side. He got in beside me, Bud and Rick behind. Back of me, upended on the back seat, was a zipper bag like mine except bigger, while on the floor in front of it was a wastebasket, a metal thing chocolate brown in color, with slots in the sides. Pal put my bag on the seat between him and me, then snapped all the door locks down, except the one back of me was already snapped down. "OK, Beautiful, when you get off the lot, turn right, then run straight ahead till I tell you to turn. You'll be taking a right."

"Right, straight ahead, then right?"

"That's it, take it away."

So I turned onto the street, which was called Wilkens Avenue, and right away Bud chirped up, "She's OK, she drives like we want."

And Pal explained to me, "What he's talking about, Beautiful, is that signal you gave. Strictly speaking, you didn't have to, from a parking lot to a street, but you did anyway, from habit, which is what we want. Because on something like this it's the little things that can trip you. You line all the big things up, and then you go through a light, or park next to a fire plug, or don't stick that flipper out—and a cop flags you down. But you do stick it out, so OK. Keep it up, you're doing fine."

We passed Colypte, and he said, "Take it easy, also slow down for a couple of blocks so you get the run of this street. This plant, it's part of this job we're pulling."

"We passed it last night on our walk."

"Then get straight how it ties in."

He said today, being the fifteenth of June, was payday at the plant, "and they pay off by check. But every one of those people, the people who work in the plant, take their check to the bank, that one beyond the light. . . ."

"We passed *it* on our walk too."

"And the bank cashes them. So what does it get for being so nice about it? It gets that some of those people, after they cash their checks, deposit some in their savings accounts. But to meet that heavy demand, the bank has extra cash, over a hundred grand, that's sent out from downtown—it came out last night, we checked, so everything's in order. . . . OK, there's your light. Now drive on past the bank. It's a branch of the Chesapeake Banking and Trust Company."

"Yes, sir. We know."

I passed the bank, which was on the corner, going slow so we could see it. But at the next corner he said, "OK, take a right and circle the block so you come up to the light on the cross-street running past the bank. There'll be something I want you to see."

So I did, coming up beside the bank and crossing with the light. And what was there, what he wanted me to see, was the phone booth I'd noticed the night before halfway up the block on the other side of the light. He said, "Do you see it, Beautiful; do you see it, Chuck?" And when we said we did, he went on, "That booth is there where it is for one and only reason: to be used by the bunch from the bank. Every morning, eight-thirty, they gather around, the tellers, the branch manager, and the guard, who in this bank wears regular clothes, with his gun in an armpit holster. They gather around it, and you'll note that from where it's located it's in view of the bank and the bank is in view of it. Then one of them goes in to sit there in front of the phone, so he has it in case of need. Then another of them goes down, unlocks the bank, and enters to check how things look inside. If everything's OK, if no one is in there waiting, he pulls down the shades on the door. They stay up during the night so the cop can see inside. So then when the shades go down, the bunch go trooping down and get ready to open the bank, open it up for the day's business. But if in thirty seconds those shades don't come down, the guy in the booth calls, and the cops get there fast."

All enduring that I'd been driving along, so I was two or three blocks past the booth, but he didn't tell me to turn till he made sure we had it straight, about the booth and how it figured in. Then he told me turn right, run back to Wilkens again, then circle around to come in past the bank the way I had the first time. He said, "Now, like before, take a right turn and stop. Right now, stop." So I did, stopping on the cross-street beyond the bank and around the corner from it. When I'd pulled up the brake, he said, "An hour from now, while they're all gathered around the booth, I'll have you stop like this so I can get out and walk back to them, fumbling my money in my moist little fist like I want to make a call. Except what I really want is to listen to what they're saying and notice how they act. They shouldn't suspicion me—after all, they won't see any car or have any idea where I came from, but if they do I want to know it. Then if everything's OK, I watch them troop down to the bank, and we know it's all clear. Or we know that it's not. Either way is important."

"All right, I have it now."

"Drive on. Get on Wilkens again."

I drove five or six blocks on Wilkens, headed east, at lease as I think, that is, toward the center of town, and when he told me to turn, I did, to my left. After some blocks he told me to turn right, and I was on a through street, a sign saying Frederick Road. He said, "OK, now, run five or six blocks, until I tell you to stop, then take a right. But in the first block of the cross-street take it slow—there's something else for you to look at."

I did just as he said, but all I could see was the end of an alley that ran in between the block, parallel to Frederick Road. But it turned out that was what he meant, and he told me, "Cast your eye up the alley; slow down as you pass and look up it. Tell me what you see."

". . . Blue car is all. Blue sedan."

"That's right. That's what we're looking for. Now stop and let me out, then half-circle the block to stop at the far end of the alley. I'll meet you there, but if I don't show, Bud'll take over, and you'll do whatever he says."

"Yes, sir."

"I'm having a look at that car."

So he dropped off and I half-circled the block, but when I drove to the alley's end, he came out of it, and when I stopped he got in. He had me do it all over again, turn into the cross-street I'd turned into the first time, but this time made me turn into the alley and park back of the blue. He said, "It's all clear in the other car, no stakeout waiting or anything, but I want you to have it down pat, how to park, how to do it quick, so we can switch cars fast, with no hang-ups." So I did it all as he said, slipping in back of the blue, setting the brake, checking distances, and so on. He said, "Took us two weeks to find this spot, but it's worth its cover in hundred-dollar bills. The beauty part is those buildings, the ones on each side of the alley. They none of them have back windows. With luck we'll make our switch without being seen by *anyone*, and then we just vanish. No one sees us, no one catches our number, no one has anything on us."

Rick asked, "That car, is it hot?"

"Chuck, both of us have cars, Bud and I, up north

where we live, but on something like this you dare not use your own. Yes, the car's hot. This car is hot. Both cars are hot."

". . . Where do I come in?"

"Don't worry, I'm coming to you."

By now I was back on Frederick, so we were headed back where we had started from. Pal went on: "OK, Chuck, now let's get *you* straightened out. Your job is a double job. You hold the basket, this one in front of the seat, while the girl pitches money in it. I'll pick one of the girls, one of the woman tellers, and make her handle the money. And while you're doing that you'll watch her feet, that she don't play us tricks. We face all kinds of dangers, but one of them is the floor, which has all kinds of stuff on it, triggers and buttons and pedals, that she can kick and that will bring in the cops. So that's your double job, to hold the basket at her, while she pitches the money in, and watch her feet like a hawk, that she doesn't play us tricks. OK, then, so you both get the picture: soon as I see them go down from the phone booth to the bank, and count 'em and join up again in the car, we go have ourselves something to eat, sandwich or bun or whatever, and a cup of coffee to calm us down. Then, nine-thirty, we drive back to the bank and Beautiful parks out front. She stays there while we're inside. Then Bud goes in and throws the gun down on them all— makes them put up their hands and line up in a row. Then we come in, you and I, Chuck, me with my drawn gun, you with the basket here, this one that you see on the floor. I make the tellers open their carts, or buggies, as they're called. They're rollaway carts, little cabinets on wheels, with steel drawers in them, that they keep right at their sides, in under the shelf back of their windows. Each teller has his own key, and each drawer opens separate. I call them up one by one and make them do it quick. Then one by one I send them out in the middle, where Bud takes charge of them—makes them lie on the floor, face down, with their hands stretched in front of their heads. When the carts are all open I call up the girl, the one that you're to watch, and she goes down the line, opens the cart drawers, throws the money into your basket, and then when she's done, goes out and lies down with the others. If, while we're doing all that, customers happen to come, Bud takes care of them, making them lie down too. When the girl is done, we're done, and boy, we get out of there fast. You first, Chuck, with the basket, me next, and Bud last, still covering that bunch on the floor. We hop in the car and Beautiful gives it the gas. Then in the car we transfer it, the dough you've got in the basket, to the bag here that you see, so we can handle it easy. Then Beautiful pulls in to the other car, we switch both bags to it, then *out*. And then we split in the car, say good-bye, and that's that. Everything clear, now?"

"What do I do if she *does* make a pass with her feet?"

"You grab her, that's what."

"How can I, with both hands holding the basket?"

Pal was annoyed, but Bud said, "It's a point, don't smack it out. With both his hands full it could mean that second's delay that could ruin us."

"OK, Chuck, take a one-hand grip on the basket."

"I can't if it starts getting heavy."

They figured on that for a while, everyone quite

annoyed, and then Bud said, "Can't he kick her? Fetch her one in the shins? If she gets wandering feet?"

Rick said: "OK, that ought to do it."

Pal asked him, "How do you feel?"

"I feel good, Mr. Pal."

"He don't look so good."

That was Bud, and Pal twisted around so he was facing Rick. Then: "Chuck, are you all right?"

"I said I felt good. Yeah, I'm OK."

"You're kind of pasty under the eyes."

"It's something I have now and then when I'm nervous, like I want to throw up. It don't mean anything."

I said, "Rick, how you do is swallow."

"Beautiful, you're talking to Chuck."

"Oh, that's right, I'm sorry."

For some time nothing was said, and I kept driving along. Then Pal asked Bud, "What do you think?"

"I think we do or we don't."

"OK, then. We do."

6

At 8:25 exactly, with Rick still doing his best and hanging on somehow, I stopped on the cross-street after driving past the bank and taking the right turn. Pal got out and walked back, and I commenced watching behind, for what I could see on Wilkens, through the rear window, though the bag standing up in between made it I had to stretch my neck. But there was nothing to see, and I told Bud, "There's no traffic back there—on foot, of people walking, or out in the street, of cars." He said, "Yeah, this time of day things are slack. We took note of that already. It's another thing in our favor." I said it over again to Rick, hoping it might relax him, so the nervousness might pass, and it seemed to help, just a little. Anyhow, he said, "Yeah, Mandy, that's good." Then Bud snapped at him that I was Beautiful, and Rick said, "Yeah, that's right, I forgot." In ten minutes, though it seemed a lot longer than that, Pal was back, telling me, "OK,

Beautiful, drive on." Bud said, "OK, spill it, what happened?"

"Nothing, nothing at all. I walked up like I wanted to the booth, counting the silver in my hand, and the guy inside nodded, holding up one finger, meaning he'd only be a minute. I stepped aside, like I was not in any hurry, and a girl went on talking about what a chance one of the downtown tellers was taking, shacking up with her boss weekends at a motel. She paid no attention to me and none of them did. It's just like we hoped it would be."

"How many of them were there?"

"Ah, eight."

But he kind of hesitated and Bud caught it, turning into a wolf. "Goddam it, how many?" he screamed. You'd never have thought they were friends—if they were, which I'm not so sure of now.

"I told you, didn't I? Eight?"

"You did but you don't seem sure!"

"I'm sure. There were eight."

"You counted them?"

"Of course I did! What was I there for?"

"I'd damn well like to know."

I asked, "Mr. Pal, where do I go?"

"Frederick Road, then I'll show you."

Where Pal showed me was to a Holiday Inn, but we no sooner were brought to a table than he took Rick downstairs, to run his finger down his throat, or at lease so I supposed, and what he did do I don't know, but when he came back he looked better. Then we all had buns and coffee, except Rick didn't eat anything, just sipped along on his coffee. But while they were gone Bud was growling. "You heard what he said, didn't you, Beautiful? About the girl? Shacking up with her boss at a motel, like that was a hot bit for us? So if that's what they're rapping about, they don't have their mind on us, and no stakeout is there. So OK, the deep stuff is in, we got it covered complete! But the one thing I have to know, which is how many of them pigeons there are, he can't be bothered about. He's so goddam busy with this other, the chick shacking up in the motel, that he forgets to count. Listen, I got to know and I don't! He said eight, but, Christ, he wasn't sure!" It cleared up a point that baffled the cops, as I'll explain in due course, when I get to it later on, but right now one thing at a time.

Pal left a tip and paid the cashier, and then we were driving again, headed for the bank. At 9:29 sharp, I pulled up in front and set the brake. Pal said, "OK, this is it."

"I don't want to."

Rick kind of whined it, but Pal reached back and shook his knee. Very cold, he said, "Chuck, you got to."

"I don't want to. I want out."

"Chuck, you're in."

"...OK."

He just whispered it. Bud got out and went in the bank. Pal got out. Rick got out, then reached in and picked up the basket. Pal told me, "Beautiful, set the doors so they open quick but aren't hanging wide for some cop to get sore about."

"I'll set them right, don't worry."

He and Rick went in, Rick carrying the basket, and I had a look at the street to see what was moving on it, but nothing was. No cars were coming toward me, and none were backed up behind, waiting for the light. At the end of the block a girl was walking along in the direction of the bank but not paying attention to me. I slid over, pushing my bag on the seat, to set the doors, pulling both of them in, so they looked to be closed but weren't. The door catches weren't caught, and they'd open at any pull. I slid back of the wheel again, pulling the bag beside me, and checked my motor to make sure that I still had it. It was humming along nice. The girl was still the only thing moving, that I could see, in the block, and by now she had reached the bank. She went in and my heart skipped a beat. But then I remembered: the way they were going to work it, she was under control. She would be made to lie down and wouldn't cause any louse-up. From behind, after crossing with the light, a man came along and went in. But except for him, there was still no traffic at all, going or coming on Wilkens, or, that I could see, on the side street.

Then from inside the bank came a shot.

It sounded faint, and what with the motor running and me being inside the car, I wasn't quite sure what it was. But then came another, and then two or three more, so there couldn't be any mistake. For the first time my stomach felt queer. I was afraid, and my toe wanted the gas, to slam that car out of there. However, I made myself hold. Behind me, out of the corner of my eye, I could see the light turn red, but still no cars were there. There may have been more shots, I can't be sure, but then all of a sudden out of the bank came Rick, staggering under the weight of the basket, which seemed to be full. But he was carrying it funny, by one hand, reaching back over his shoulder so it was on his back in a hunched-up, clumsy way. I opened the door, the front door, and he fell in, the basket on top of him and his legs hanging out the door. Then he pulled them in and as he did, said to me, "Mandy! Out of here! Quick! Step on it!"

"But where are Pal and Bud?"

"They're dead, they're shot. Who the hell cares where they are? Mandy, will you get going? Will you get us the hell out of here?"

I started, then saw that the door was still open. I said, "Rick! Will you close the door? Will you pull it shut? Will you slam it?"

He tried to but was wedged in on the floor, the basket on top of him, his legs sticking up in the air, so he couldn't move. And money, packs of ones and fives and tens and twenties, done up in rubber bands, in paper tape, and loops of string, were all over the floor, fouling my gas and clutch and brake. But somehow, at last, I got to the corner and turned right to get out of sight, when, thank God, the door swung shut though it didn't slam, and when I looked, the back door was closed though not slammed shut. As I turned the light was still red, but still no cars were there. A guy ran out of the bank, but I pulled ahead and out of his sight. At the next corner I turned right again, to double back in the direction we'd been in. Rick was still on the floor, but he felt what I was doing and started to wail. I said, "It's OK, if anything's on our tail, it's the last thing they'd expect."

I ran two blocks with no cars showing behind, then caught open country, or vacant lots anyhow, on both sides of the road, with no one in sight. I stopped, jumped out, ran around, and yanked open both doors. I grabbed the basket, and it was almost too much for me, too heavy for me to lift. But I wrapped both arms around it and pushed it in back, on the floor in front of the seat, the way it had been in the first place, as far over as I could slide it. Then I pulled him out by the feet. I told him, "Get in there! Get in back, quick!" I wanted him in with the money, and at lease he did what I said. I slammed both doors, ran around again and got in, then started up. I ran a block or two, then cut back and got on Wilkens. I was near the Colypte plant but ran past it to the bank, and soon as the light turned, past it. A squad car was out front, an officer standing beside it, talking into a mike, with people gathered around, maybe fifteen or twenty. One or two of the men, who had on gray cotton jackets, looked to be from the bank. As I passed, no one paid any attention to me, and Rick kept whispering, "What do you know about that? What do you know about that?"

"Now, at last we can talk! What happened?"

"What didn't happen! My God!"

I realized he still couldn't talk and didn't press him too hard, then turned left, to head for Frederick—Frederick Road I'm talking about. But then I suddenly realized I didn't quite know where I was and went in to ask at the next filling station I came to. I almost died when the guy reached for my door handle to throw off the lock on the hood, because that stuff was still lying around, the money, on the floor, where it had fallen out of the basket and I'd kicked it away from my pedals. I slapped my hand over the door and said, "Oil's OK, thanks. Fill her up—it'll take six, I think." So he turned from the door to the hose, and as he opened the tank a

TV started to talk, from the other side of the car, inside the filling station: "... All three men were dead on arrival at University of Maryland Hospital, both of the bandits and Lester Bond, the guard, whom one of the bandits shot after being shot himself, taking aim from the floor...." I asked for Frederick Road, after paying for my gas, and when I had straight where I was, I drove on. I said, "Rick, did you hear him? That announcer on TV? Not only Pal and Bud, but the bank guard, *he*'s dead too."

"I heard him. That's bad."

"I still don't know what happened."

At last he started to talk: "You know how they had it lined up? Well, that's exactly how they did it, and it went like it was greased. A girl came in and Bud made her lie down out there by the customers' desk, and when a guy came in, he made him do the same. Then, soon as Pal handled the tellers, making them open those carts, they marched right out to Bud and lay down beside the girl, the one on the floor already. Then the girl that Pal picked out to pitch the money in, she commenced doing her stuff, me holding the basket for her until it was almost full and getting so heavy I was wondering if I could hang on to it. Then she went out and lay down, and Pal and I went out through the gate, the one in the railing that runs across the bank from the tellers' windows, in front of a bunch of desks that the secretaries sit at. And Pal said to me, 'OK, Chuck, *out*! To the car, shove the dough in, get in, and wait!'

"That he half-whispered, but Bud cut in on him quick: 'I got ten people here on the floor, two from outside and eight from the bank, but not no goddam guard!' He roared it and kept on: 'Not no guy with a gun! Where the hell did he go? *Where is he?'*

"Well he found out soon enough.

"He was still roaring at Pal when a guy popped out of a door, one that leads to rooms in back, his face all lathered up except one side was shaved, a razor in his hand and a gun under his arm, with straps running off from the holster, over his shoulder and around his chest. The look on his face said he'd come at the sound of Bud's roaring, from shaving himself in the men's room. Bud saw him and fired, but not soon enough. Because soon as he saw what was up, he ducked back of the railing and then leveled his gun on it, using it for a gun rest so he could sight. He fired and Bud went down. By that time Pal was firing his gun from the other side of the bank. But he had no target to shoot at and almost at once fell. And then, Mandy, I had the worst moment of my whole life, as I woke up that I would be next. I dropped the basket and started to run. But then I knew I had to have it, for protection so I wouldn't be killed, to keep it between me and him, between my back and the gun. I grabbed it by one hand and muscled it onto my back, then started running again. And he started shooting again. I could feel the *chock* of bullets and hear their *zing* as they hit the tin, but none of them went through, thank God. I made the door and got out, and know nothing about the rest, him being shot by Pal, if Pal was the one that did it, or any of it, except me falling into the car, still holding the basket to me so I wouldn't be hit by the shots."

He stopped and I kept driving on, but pretty soon I told him, "Bud was sore about it, Pal messing up the count of the bunch there at the phone booth. It's all he talked about at the Holiday Inn while you were away from the table."

"He had reason to be."

By now I was close to the cross-street that the alley ended on, and I said, "Rick, we'll have to switch cars pretty soon, so will you transfer the money? From the basket to the bag? So we can carry it?"

"Mandy, to hell with the money! Let's get out of here! Let's, for Christ's sake, not have any retakes of that nightmare there in the bank, when I thought I was going to die! Let's ditch this car, blow, and wipe today out if we can!"

"You mean walk off and leave the money?"

"It's hot! It can get us the gas chamber! That guard is dead, and they can pin it on us! It's not who did it, it's who was in it!"

"Then, OK, get out!"

". . . What did you say?"

"I say if that's all the nerve you got, then get out, *git*! But I'm not getting out! I'm not leaving this dough! It's ours and I mean to keep it!"

"Who says I don't have any nerve?"

"I do! You've lost any nerve that you did have!"

"Listen, there's more to it than you know about!"

"Yeah? Like what?"

"Like what they were fixing to do—*to us*!"

"*Who* was fixing to do?"

"Those two guys that got killed!"

"And what were they fixing to do?"

"To kill us, that's what!"

He said he'd caught Bud drawing his finger over

_____ 49 _____

his throat, when he thought he wasn't looking, and Pal nodding his head. He said, "They meant to let us have it, right here in this car, before they made the switch. That's the split they intended to make. That's what they meant to do!"

"Funny *I* didn't catch on."

"Or maybe they didn't mean you. Maybe, for you, Pal had different ideas. Maybe the both of them did."

"What different ideas?"

"What do you think?"

". . . Rick, you shoving off or not?"

But instead of getting out, he pushed the bag down so it was standing right-side up on the back seat where he was, instead of being upended in front of the window. Then he opened it, cocking the hinges so it wouldn't fold shut. He began transferring the money, pitching it in from the basket, every which way, without bothering to pack it neat. When he got done the bag was nearly full and he snapped it shut. I said, "OK, but I've run past our turn, the one I take for the alley. We're in West Baltimore. I'll have to run back."

So I did, circling around, taking four or five turns. Then at last I came to the cross-street, turned into it, then turned into the alley. The blue was still there and I parked behind it, just as I had before. I set the brake and got out, taking the key ring. I walked to it, peeped inside to make sure no one was there, and unlocked it. I got in, tried the new key in the ignition to make sure it would turn on. It did and I started the motor. Rick tapped on the right-hand window, and I threw the lock to let him get in. But he reached around inside the front door, undid the lock on the rear door, opened it, and put the bag on the back seat. Then he got in beside me, locking both right-hand doors. But he hadn't brought my bag. I got out and went back to get it. And when I opened the driver's door to take it from the front seat, that money was still there, that bunch of ones, fives, tens, and twenties that had spilled out when Rick got in, to be under my feet, in the way. I grabbed them up and stuffed them into my handbag. Then I went back to the blue and got in. As I pulled away Rick asked, "Where do we go from here?"

"Well, one thing at a time, let me think."

"Well, where *do* we go from here?"

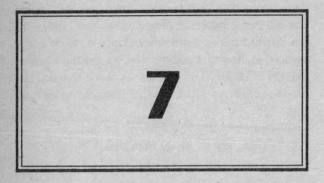

7

He said it pretty peevish, and I had no answer yet, as I'd been so busy driving, making him transfer the money, and switching cars in the alley to figure on it at all. Now I tried to, still driving around, at lease as well as I could, but he was no great help, talking along some more in his peevish, fault-finding way: "We can't go to a motel because look what happened last night—we had hardly got in the door before they commenced suspicioning us, and with this heavy bag in my hand they might want to know what's in it. So what are we going to say? Suppose they tell us open it up; what are we going to do? OK, so they *don't* tell us open it up, but that leaves us worse off than before. They give us a room but those places all have maids, and the one on our floor, she wouldn't be human if she didn't wonder about this bag. And when we go out to eat, you think she's got too many principles to open it up and peep? It's unlocked and we can't lock it, as we don't have any key. Maybe those guys had one, but they're unfortunately dead now and it doesn't do us any good. We wouldn't dare go out, to get something to eat or do anything else! Go out, hell! We dare not go to a motel or anywhere! And we dare not stay in this car—it's hot, as we know, they told us. And sooner or later, at some bridge or tunnel or light, a cop will hold up his hand, look in his little book, find our number, and that'd be that. In Maryland murder's murder—it's not whether you used the gun. Being in it is enough."

"Well, at lease, you didn't want to be."

"You know why I wanted out?"

"They meant to plug you, you said."

"Yeah, that was nice, wasn't it? First they're going to plug you, then they get shot so they can't. Then the guard starts shooting at you, and then he gets plugged so he can't. Now it's the gas chamber, that's all."

"Rick, you want out or not?"

"Mandy, what next? What are we going to do?"

He was losing his nerve fast, if he hadn't already lost it, and maybe I felt funny too, but one thing I knew, I was not going to chicken now, run off as he seemed to want, leaving the money here in the car. So I kept driving around trying to think and pretty soon saw a shopping plaza, a big place off to our right, with all kinds of stores in it. I said, "OK, Rick, how's this? So the bag is un-locked, and we dare not go to a motel for fear of that nosy maid who'll open it up and see the money. So how about going in here? Putting the car in their park, going in one of the stores, using some of the money, and buying a new bag to hold it, a suitcase with a lock and a key that we have, then bringing the bag to the car, putting the money in it, locking it up and taking the key, then leaving the car and taking the bag in a taxi to the bus terminal, where we check it to leave it? We keep the key and the check, and that's that for as long as we want. We're rid of it, so we get time to think. Then, to do our thinking in, we go to a motel like before, except I say we go to a hotel."

"Why a hotel?"

"Motel's for people with cars, and we'll be using a cab. And besides, in a hotel they treat you better. They got bellboys that carry your bag."

"That new bag will be just as heavy from the money we'll be putting in it. Suppose the guy in the bus terminal wants to know why?"

"In the bus terminal do they care?"

"Well? I was just asking."

"They handle hundreds of bags every day, and to them one bag looks like another. All they want is your money."

"Well, OK, I was just asking!"

But he didn't sound quite so peevish, and I asked, "Then is that what we're going to do? Are we set?"

"Then, yeah."

"Then let's do it."

"And cut out the talking, you mean?"

"That's it, Rick, Now you've said it."

"There's one other thing then."

"Which is? Let's get *everything* out!"

"We could buy ourselves a couple of bags. Suit-cases, I'm talking about. If I had one, I could buy some stuff like shirts, so I wouldn't smell so bad. I'd have something to carry them in. And your bag's not so hot—a new one and you could leave it right here in the car. Then with new bags and stuff, even a nice hotel wouldn't ask us to pay in advance."

"You mean you're with it?"

"Well, we might as well go in style."

"Then we're set."

So that's what we did, though he still didn't sound like he had too much of a yen, and wound up a couple hours later in a big hotel downtown, which I don't name as I mix hotels up and might get the wrong one. Anyway, it was as nice as they come, and our room was something to see, with light-green carpet real thick, fine, comfortable furniture, and a bathroom to dream about. From our shopping tour of the plaza, we each had our own small suitcase that I'd repacked my own things into and that he packed his things into, that he bought in the men's store and I paid for out of the money I had, that I'd picked up from the floor of the car, the first one, before we switched to the blue. But he still wasn't showing much interest, in me or anything, and while I was putting the things away, mine at first and then his, in my bureau drawer and his, he lay down on the bed. When I asked what was the trouble, he said, "Same old thing, Mandy. Thing like that, you don't get over it quick—I mean knowing I had to die. Knowing I was helping them get rich and that then they meant to kill me."

"Well? So they got killed. Served them right."

"Yeah, that's easy to say."

"Would you like to be alone? Kind of rest a while?"

"Mandy! It's what I wanted to ask!"

"OK. I'll go down and have some lunch."

"...Can I have a drink sent up?"

"Well, of course. But don't get slopped up, Rick. I don't like guys when they're slopped. They...just don't appeal to me."

"I never take but one. But, Mandy, I need it."

"Then have it! Of course!"

So I went down, feeling suddenly hungry, as it was going on one and I'd had nothing to eat since the bun in the Holiday Inn. I headed for the coffee shop, which was out of this world, a beautiful place with pretty girls in pink uniforms, and had a tongue sandwich with pickles and olives, buttermilk, which I love, and, of course, apple pie a la mode. It was wonderful; the pie was so thick, and the apples kind of scrunchy, from being not quite cooked, so they were tart and tasty. So while I was eating I saw a boy come into the lobby, dump papers down by the newsstand, and go out. When I got there, the man was cutting the rope and I bought one, then bought another for Rick. Then I went back to the table and started to read. So there I was, holding the key and the check in my bag (the new handbag that I'd bought) to the $120,000 suitcase, the amount the story said had been taken in the holdup. I own up it made me feel funny, not as funny as Rick, maybe, but pretty nervous just the same, as I read all the details, which had according-tos, it-is-allegeds, and stuff like that mixed in, but corresponding in all that mattered to what Rick had said in the car. And it turned out that Bud was right in suspicioning Pal's count of the bunch at the telephone booth— that the right number was nine instead of eight. Because the guard needed a shave, expecting to have it at lunch, but the manager made him take it at once. So that explained quite a lot, but I kept on feeling funny. Then, however, I didn't feel funny at all but turned on in a way I'd never been in my life. And why I was turned on was the girl, the one who had handled the money, had made a positive idemnification of "the boy who held the basket," from mug shots the police showed her, as Vito Rossi, "one of the mob." It turned out that this was a famous four, known as the Caskets from the number of funerals they'd caused and from the name of the head bandit, Matt Caskey. His picture was there, the one who had called himself Pal, and Bud's picture was there, over the name Howie Hyde. But two other pictures were there: the Rossi brothers, Vito and Vanny, and, sure enough, one of them did favor Rick, though if you ask me, all boys with long hair look alike. Anyway, it meant that no one had any idea, any idea at all, that Rick and I were in it, or even that a girl was driving the car, because that's what it said in there, that the police "conjectured" that Vanny was driving the getaway car as usual, though no one had actually seen him.

That's what turned me on.

I thought, "We've got away with it clean!"

I thought, "You can have that mink coat; it's yours, it's yours! All you need do is go buy it!"

So I did.

I threw both papers away, passed through the lobby, went outside, and had the doorman whistle me up a cab. I'd given him a buck when we came and gave him fifty cents now, and when I got in I asked for department stores. The driver said, "There's a whole flock of them, Miss, at Howard and Lexington streets," and he mentioned Hutzler's, Stewart's, and Hochschild Kohn, though like with the hotels I'm always mixing them up, at lease the Baltimore ones, so I will not say which one it was he set me down in front of. Whichever it was, I went in and asked for the fur coat department, and, lo and behold, they were having a sale on coats, marked down fifteen percent from what they had been in winter, and I didn't mind at all. So for the next hour I lived. I had them show me coats and coats and coats, beautiful ones in all kinds of different colors, like Scotch Mist and Pastel Beige, but I didn't take anything fancy. I like the natural mink, and I finally took a fingertip thing, a beautiful full brown, with wide sleeves and a collar to wear two ways, up around my neck or flat out on my shoulders. So it was $1,600 and I paid with twenties, breaking the tapes on two packs of bills. I said, "I'm spending my wedding present." The woman stared and said, "Well, what's your name, please? So I can have the monogram put in beside the label, in the inside pocket." I said, "Never mind the monogram, please. I'm in a bit of a hurry and don't want to wait while it's done." I didn't give my name and got out of there pretty quick. However, nobody stopped me or tried to follow me that I could see.

The store had a doorman too, and I gave him fifty cents to get me another cab and told the driver the address on Lombard Street, which I didn't have to look up, as after last night I'd never forget it. But then, riding along, it all looked strangely familiar, and it turned out, when I asked the driver, that I'd been there that very morning, as Lombard Street runs into Frederick Road. It all seemed very queer, but when we got to the block the house was in, I had him stop and wait on the corner so he couldn't hear what was going to be said. I walked to the house in the coat, thanking God the day wasn't hot or I'd have looked like a kook. It was just a Baltimore house, two-story, of brick, with green shutters and white marble steps, and I went up and rang the bell. A child opened the door, a little boy. I said, "Mr. Vernick, please."

". . . My father's eating his lunch."

"Please tell him it's important."

Then a woman was there, in housedress and gingham apron. She asked, "Who are you? What do you want?"

"I want to see Mr. Vernick."

"I asked who you are."

"Ok, but who are you?"

"I'm Mrs. Vernick. Once more, who are you?"

Her voice had an ugly sound all of a sudden, and maybe mine did too as I told her. "I'm *Miss* Vernick— his daughter, Mandy."

"He doesn't have any daughter."

"Oh yes he has. I'm her."

There may have been more, I'm not sure. But in the middle of it, here a guy came in his shirt-sleeves, a youngish guy in his thirties, with long nose and eyes set close together. He put his arms around the woman, kissed her, then stepped in front of her and the child, though they both stuck around to hear. He asked, "Yes, Miss? What can I do for you?"

"You're Edward Vernick?"

"That's right. Who are you?"

"I'm your daughter, Mandy. I talked to you last night, and you said some things I have to go further with. Like insinuating I would ask you for money."

"I don't have any daughter."

"Don't you think my mother knows?"

"Who is your mother, please?"

"Sally Vernick, your former wife."

"... It's true, Sally Vernick was my wife, or at least we were married for quite a few years, though we actually lived together five days. But, Mandy, you're not my child, as I can pretty well prove."

"Pretty well? What does *that* mean?"

"Means until now, I don't have actual proof."

I piled into him for that, though liking it less and less, as it was beginning to bug me bad that I didn't like this guy or want him for a father. So I said stuff, pretty mean, finally asking, "And what does *that* mean, 'until now'?"

"Means that now at last, when I see what you look like, Mandy, there's no resemblance at all to me or my kith or my kin." That's what he said, "kith or kin." He went on: "If I ever had any doubt of the trick your mother played me in naming me as your father, I don't have anymore. You're not my child, Mandy, so let's get it over with, what you came about. You said something about money. Is that what this is, a touch?"

None of it was going as I'd hoped, and in fact I was caught by surprise by that stuff he was dishing out, which seemed to say, and in fact did say, that someone else was my father, so my tongue kind of got stuck, and words wouldn't come, or at lease the kind of words I wanted. But now all of a sudden words did come, of the very kind I wanted. I flung the coat around, saying, "Does *this* look like a pauper? Does it look like I need your money?"

"Does *what* look like you need my money?"

"This coat, what do you think?"

"Well, it's a very nice coat."

"I asked if it looks like I need your money?"

"Mandy, it doesn't look like anything, until I know how you got it. How did you get it, then?"

"Is that any of your business?"

"It is if I'm to answer your question. Was it given you? And if so, by whom? Or did you steal it? Or did you get it the way your mother got hers? If she has one."

"What do you mean, the way she got hers?"

"You know what I mean—*in bed*."

"How'd you like to go to hell?"

"Was there something else?"

8

I must have got back in the cab and ridden down to the hotel, but the next thing I really remember is bursting into the room, after opening the door with my key, and coming apart all over, right in front of Rick. He was in bed in pajamas, a highball tray beside him, reading the paper, the same one I had read, that he'd had sent up with the Scotch and seltzer and ice. And I no sooner was there than I started to whoop, weeping and wailing and bawling, so I couldn't make myself stop. And then in the middle of it I saw tears on the coat and whipped it off so it wouldn't get smeared up and threw it on the other bed. Then I went on with the show. He lay there staring at me, then got up to stare at the coat, then walked to the chair in his bare feet to sit and listen at me. Then after a long time he asked, "OK, what have you done? Are they on your tail or what? And where did this coat come from?" It was some time before I could speak, but then I said, "I haven't done anything! It's that Vernick, the things that he said! The lying things, the rotten things, to me, out there at his house!" So then I started to talk as control came at last, while he sat there, listening to what I said.

It went on quite a while. Because I no sooner started on Vernick than I'd have to backtrack to the store to explain about the coat. And I'd no sooner get started on that than I'd have to backtrack to lunch and what I'd seen in the paper. And then, all of a sudden, I started crying again—for no reason at all, but I did. So at last he started to talk. He said, "That's nice, I'll say it is. Here we were inching ahead—bought ourselves bags, checked the big one to leave it, then found ourselves a pad so we could lay up and think. Then we really got a break. Mandy, did you read *all* the stuff in the paper? How that girl identified me? As Vito Rossi, one of the bandit mob? We didn't know it, but this was the worst bunch of thugs on earth, the Caskets, and Rossi, he was one of them. And the girl, the one that forked over the money, when shown a picture of him, a mug shot by the police, said, 'Yes, that's the one, *he* held the basket.' We were all in the clear, playing in wonderful luck, and then what do you do? Go and buy this coat, paying with twenty-dollar bills that *had* to be hot. The store still has them and is going to report them, sure as God made little apples, to the police, who of course report to the papers. And as though that wasn't enough, you parade the damned coat for Vernick, and when *he* sees the papers, that's it!.... Christ, we had it made! It was all ours. We were in the clear. And now what? If the eight ball was there before, God knows what the number is now!" And he fell on his knees in front of the chair, burying his face in the seat.

"You don't have to cry about it."

"How stupid can you get?"

"At lease I did something! I didn't just lie there, drinking booze and feeling sorry for myself!"

He got back into bed again and lay there a long time. Then, moaning, he kept saying over and over, "Mandy, how could you? How could you?"

"... OK then, I did wrong."

"Here we were sitting pretty, and..."

"I did what I had to do! It was why I got in it at all! To get this mink coat and shake it in his face, that horrible Ed Vernick! I told you, didn't I? I told you, I told those bandits!"

"Oh, for Christ's sake, shut up!"

He got back into bed, then lay there a while, pressing his hands to his head and squirming under the covers. Then at last he sat up and commenced hollering again. "I have to find out! If that *goddam* store called the *cops*! I have to find out and I can't—I can't go out to call; I don't have any pants! I sent them out, sent them out with the coat to be pressed, to be dry-cleaned and pressed, and here I am caught with no clothes till that valet brings them back. *And I got to find out!*"

"You mean you're going to ask them, 'Did you call the cops?' Oh, boy! Talk about *me* being dumb!"

"No, I know what I'm going to ask, but..."

"Well, can't you call from here?"

"And have these girls listen in?"

"Rick, get with it, for God's sake. Wake up where you are! You could be president of the United States and these girls would not listen in! They're too busy! This place is too big! It's..."

"OK, OK."

He grabbed the coat, which was still on the other bed, turned the pocket down to look at the label, and when he had the name of the store found the number in the book. He gave it in, and when the store came on he said, "Fur coat department, please.... Fur coats? Did a girl come in today to buy a mink coat off you? Young girl around sixteen, paying with twenty-dollar bills?... Oh, she did! Well, I'm her husband, and I just called to say I'm bringing that coat back! She had no business buying a mink coat at all! That money was given to us, to both of us when we got married, for sheets and blankets and carpets and chairs, to help furnish our home!... What did you say?" Then he held on for some time and listened while some woman talked at the other end. Then, in kind of a different tone, he said, "Then, you won't take it back? OK, it's what I wanted to know." He hung up, fell back on the bed, and gasped, "Thank God, thank God, thank God!"

"Yeah? For what?"

"They haven't called the cops—I could tell from how she talked, that woman who came on the line. She said money was money, and it wasn't up to them to ask any questions about it. She said the girl did mention her wedding present, but if that much cash was unusual, there was nothing about it that the store had to question at all or pass judgment on. And merchandise on sale is not subject to return. *And*, she gave me no lead at all to find out who I was or bait me into the store. All she gave me was the brush. *So*..."

"Seems that God *didn't* make little apples—just big ones, maybe."

"Now there's a thought. There's a thought and a half."

He squirmed in the bed some more, then burst out, "I've got to find out about Vernick! Whether he called the cops, or what! I've got to check on him!"

So he looked in the book again and gave the number in that I knew so well. Then: "Mr. Vernick, you don't know me, but I'm calling about a girl who was out to your house today, or so I understand..." Then a voice cut him off and there came a click. He hung up and said, "Thank God, thank God once more, thank the all-merciful God. He didn't call any cops either. If he had, he'd have tried to find out who I was, where I was calling from, and where Mandy Vernick was. He didn't—just said, 'I've nothing to say about her. Good-bye!'"

"So you got all worked up over nothing."

"I'm sorry, Mandy."

"And we *are* sitting pretty, aren't we?"

"*If* we are."

"Well? Are we or aren't we?"

"I don't know, I don't know! Mandy, I'm shot."

"... You mean... *you got hit*?"

"I mean I'm jittered. Bad."

"Oh! You scared me there for a minute."

At last I calmed down, then took off my clothes and went marching around naked. Then I put my pajamas on and got in the other bed. Sitting pretty or not, I felt like holy hell and wanted arms around me. I own up he didn't turn me on, at lease not much, but any port in a storm, and I'd been through one. I was hoping he'd come to me, and if it meant that other, then, OK, I'd even have stood for that. But nothing happened. I didn't know why, especially after that pass that he'd made the night before, talking about my legs and then making a pest of himself to get me in bed with him. He just lay there, now and then sipping his drink. He wasn't drunk, and he wasn't taking too much, but he seemed to need it, the way he was acting. He said he'd ordered it up from room service, along with the afternoon paper, and signed for it, tipping the boy out of the money I'd given him while we were buying our things at the plaza. He had put the tray on the luggage rack, the sawhorse thing with tapes, and offered me a drink, but I told him I didn't like it. So it went on for some little time, him sipping and thinking and me sighing and hoping, and then all of a sudden I knew why he was not coming over, not slipping into my bed when he must have known I'd say yes. It was because he was scared, or "shot" as he called it—not on account of me, of *that*, or of anything in particular, but of everything, especially the cops. And I thought about last night, the way I'd thought about it, on account of being mad. And I realized if a girl gets mad enough, she won't, and if a guy gets scared enough, he can't.

After a long time, he said, "Mandy, I've been thinking about it, 'specially about him, this guy today, Vernick. I mean he could be right. Maybe he's not your father."

"He has to be! He and mother were married!"

"That don't prove anything."

"Well, why wouldn't he be?"

"He told you. He knows stuff, of course, that he didn't mention to you, but on top of that your looks told him, so he said. You don't look like his kith or kin."

"What's kith?"

"I don't rightly know. Friends, maybe."

"His friends could be my father? Was *that* it?"

"Mandy, I don't know what it was."

"Well, what was he getting at?"

"That some other guy is your father."

"Oh! *That's* all!"

"Mandy, it could be true. And it would help, I would think, if you got with it now, 'stead of cussing him out about it."

"You mean if I *believed* it?"

"Well? I believe it."

". . . *You* believe it? Why?"

"The stuff you told me, Mandy, about yourself, about your mother, about him, and about Steve, this guy who beat you up who seemed to know more, to know a whole lot more, than he was telling you."

"And it's supposed to make me feel better?"

"At lease you'd quit plaguing yourself about him."

"But then I wouldn't know! Who my father is!"

"I was coming to that."

For the third time I'd been hit in the stomach and started to cry again. When I could talk I said, "Here it's all I've thought about, this last year and a half, my father, my real, sure-enough father, how I would go to him, how he'd ask me in real nice, how he'd take me in his arms, and how we'd be happy. And now look how it's turned out!" I told him then, for the first time, about the desert island and how I'd dreamed about it, that my father and I would swim there after our plane was forced down, and we'd stay there and live, eating clams and drinking coconut milk. I said, "Maybe we never would, maybe it was just silly, but I would imagine that we were there and laugh to myself about it, thinking how we would live there." He listened and didn't make any cracks, just let me talk along. Then he got out of bed and sat on the floor beside me, there between the beds, in front of the liquor tray, so his face was close to mine. Then he took my hand and kissed it. Then he said, "Mandy, why can't *I* be your father?"

"... *You!* You be my father, Rick?"

"Yeah, starting right now."

"You're not much more than a boy."

"I'm that much more than a boy that I can eat clams with you and drink coconut milk on that island we're going to have."

"You mean you're not laughing at it?"

"I mean we're going to have one!"

"... When? And *where*?"

"In Florida! *Now!* Now we know where we're going! Mandy, they have them down there! Cays, they call them—big ones, little ones, whatever size you want, some with palm trees on them, some with nothing but grass, but all of them with clams! We'll buy ourself one! We got money, haven't we?"

"Oh, Rick, you make me so happy!"

Because I knew, of course, that this was his way of doing, to kind of make it look different, his not coming in with me, as, of course, if he *was* my father he couldn't come to my bed, and it would be for that reason, not on account that he couldn't, that he didn't. So OK, I wasn't kidded. At the same time it was just what I wanted if he and I were to go on. I mean that other was *not* what I really wanted, though I would have stood for it regardless to get what he was giving me now, kisses and pats and love. So now I had what I really did want, without having to do that other. So it helped, in the most wonderful way. I said, "Rick, I think that's the nicest thing that's been said to me, that ever was said to me, in my whole life until now."

"Then OK. Now, little daughter, sleep."

"You make me want to cry. But happy."

He held me close in his arms, and next thing I knew it was dark. I whispered, "Rick, are you there?"

"Yes, Mandy. You've been asleep."

"I'm sorry. I'm kind of tired, I guess."

I looked then, and when I saw he was in his bed asked, "Did you sleep at all, Rick?"

"I guess so, little bit . . . much as I could, worried as I am. I can't help how I feel. Tomorrow, if we get out of town, if nobody stops us, I mean, if we get started for Florida, I imagine I'll feel different. Then it'll be the worry was just for nothing."

"I'm sorry I caused it, Rick."

"Listen, what's done is done, and when no harm is done, don't beat yourself over the head. That's how I look at it, Mandy."

"What time is it?"

"Well, you got the watch on. Look."

"It's five of ten."

"You hungry?"

"Rick, I hadn't thought. Yeah, little bit."

"I'll order something sent up. How you do, you call

room service. They'll get you a paper too—I think I'll have one sent up. The five-thirty if they still have one. It'll tell more than the one I have here, the same one you read, I guess."

"Have two sent up, one for me."

"What do you want to eat?"

"The identical same I had in the coffee shop—tongue sandwich, buttermilk, and apple pie a la mode. It was all wonderful, and the pie was out of this world."

"Guess that's what I'll have too."

So he called down and ordered, and then we got up. It was fun walking around in pajamas and barefoot, with no reason to worry about a swipe being made at my breastworks. He had money, as I'd given him a package of five-dollar bills there in the plaza, but when the food came he signed, giving the waiter a five-dollar tip. It was a very nice guy who said he was going to college and seemed to know we were new at hotels. So he told us what to do with the tray when we finished our supper, to put it out in the hall on the rolling table he brought, and in the night they'd come and get it. So then we ate our sandwiches, and everything tasted so good. We put the tray out, then sat talking about our island, Rick in one chair, me in the other, our bare feet curled up under us. Then I said, "Rick, there's just one thing."

"Yeah, Mandy? What?"

"Mother. I ought to call her up."

". . . Call her up? What for?"

"To tell her . . . what's been on my mind ever since I came back from talking to that rat, Vernick. Rick, I've been so ashamed to feel toward her like I did and to put what I did in that note. And the reason was that I blamed her for the way he had treated me, Vernick I'm talking about, never writing or calling me, or sending me something for Christmas. I thought it was because she'd never told him where we lived or anything. But now I know whose fault it was. I want to tell her how sorry I am for putting the blame on her."

"... Mandy, no, no, no!"

"But, Rick, why not?"

"You'll spill it to her, that's why."

"Spill what?"

"Everything!"

"Well, not about the robbery, if that's what you're talking about. Only about Vernick."

"Oh, that's all, about Vernick! Wasn't it bad enough, Mandy, that you went to him with that coat, that you bought it with hot money? It was just our dumb luck that the store didn't call the cops in and that he didn't want any trouble. Now you got to start over with a crazy call to your mother! Isn't there going to be any end to your battiness?"

"But I said I'm not going to tell her!"

"About anything, except Vernick and how you showed him the coat and how it flattened him out, with his talk about you wanting money. So she asks where you got it. What are you going to say?"

"I don't have to say anything, do I?"

"OK, you don't say anything, but she calls Vernick to ask what he knows about it. And he says you didn't tell him. And she says, 'I'm telling the cops, I have to, I dare not let it pass.' What then?"

"Well, she wouldn't do that."

"How do you know she wouldn't?"

"You seem to forget she's my mother."

"On this I wouldn't trust Jesus Christ."

"Well, that's not a nice thing to say."

"O.K., I wouldn't trust *anyone*."

"Then, I won't call. But you make me feel so guilty."

"I was easier in my mind. Now I'm not."

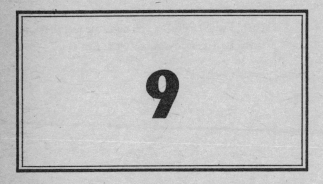

9

But in the morning we were nice and friendly again, and he let me dress in the bathroom, without peeping or anything. Then I came out and he went in, and when he came out he was shaved, combed, and fresh, with a clean shirt on, one of those he had bought, and his pants and jacket clean and pressed up, after being delivered by the valet the night before, enduring while I slept. So then we went down and had breakfast and talked over what we would do. We decided to hit for Miami, where we could ask about islands, where they were and what they cost. So we went up again and packed, then came down and paid and checked out, then took a cab to the bus terminal, at Howard and Center streets. But my heart almost stopped when we unchecked our bag, the one with the money in it, and the man suddenly asked Rick, "What you got in that thing, bricks?"

Rick told him, "Books."

"Oh, that explains it. Boy, is that heavy."

Walking away, we looked at each other, and Rick said, "Well, we found something out. Now we know what we got. In case the subject comes up. In case it does again."

"I almost died."

"Forget it. We made a gain."

But when we asked at the ticket window, it turned out that to get to Miami, to get the express bus, we had to go to Washington by local. My heart did a little more skipping when we had to surrender our bags, check them through when we got on the bus, but no comment was made anymore about how heavy the big one was. We rode on the back seat, as we had on the local from Hyattsville going to Baltimore, and I whispered to Rick, "Hiya, Pop?" He squeezed my hand, so I felt happy and loved and safe. We changed in Washington, but bought tickets only as far as Raleigh so we could have lunch there before going further south. We decided to stop in Savannah and spend the night in a hotel, before going on next day. So we did have our lunch in Raleigh, more sandwiches and pie a la mode and buttermilk, and it wasn't the same as it had been in the hotel, but not too bad either. Then we went on, with tickets bought to Savannah, checking the bags through again, riding the back seat again, and finally getting off again. And once more I almost died, as I was halfway up the aisle, leaving the bus, before I remembered the coat, which Rick had put topside on the rack. I ran back and got it and he sicked his finger at me. Then we unchecked our bags on the platform and right away rechecked the big one at the check-it-to-leave-it window, Rick taking the check that time, and then caught a cab to the hotel. Once more, I don't say which one it was, except it was down by a square, near the City Hall and Cotton Exchange, with a view looking out on some river.

They treated us very nice, very different from how they were next morning with me, and they said nothing at all about being paid in advance. We went up, and I unpacked as usual, putting our things away, and then we went out and had dinner, as it was late and the hotel dining room looked deserted. We found a place called The Isle of Hope and had a pretty good dinner of crab soup, snapper, and parfait, and with his fish Rick had some wine. Then we went back to the hotel, and I didn't undress in the bathroom, but in front of him, out in the open. But he didn't pay much attention, and I guess I liked it that way, but I was beginning to wonder how long his fright would last and if it would ever end. I mean I liked it, him being my father, but after all I'm human. But he didn't make any pass, and I sat there a while in the chair, the only one we had, and he sat sipping his Scotch, as he'd brought the bottle along, the one he'd had sent up in Baltimore. And I said, "Rick, there's just one thing."

"Yes, Mandy, what?"

"The same old. Mother.'

". . . You mean you still want to call her?"

"Rick, it's been bugging me all day. Forget what I said last night, about my reason for wanting to *then*— now there's another reason. Rick, after what you said, about her calling the cops, it was popped in my head that she could, anyway, *without* knowing about the coat. Just to report me in as a runaway girl or something. A truant juvenile, something like that. Or suppose she takes space in that magazine? They have one, did you know that? That locates missing children. And how you do, you take an ad out, give in the missing child's picture, and they run it with her description. And that magazine goes everywhere—to police, filling stations, bus terminals, airports, any place you can think of. And it gets results, so they say. The missing child is found. Well, suppose she does that to me—not out of meanness, but love. So she does what it takes to find me, and then they pick me up . . . and *you* up. And there we'll be with that money, just from being too dumb to put in a call while we still had the chance and head off that dragnet stuff. *That*'s what I'm sorried about!"

"OK, OK, I see your point. And I know what you do."

"Yes, Rick? What?"

"Soon as we get to Miami you send five bucks to New York, to the newsstand at Grand Central Station, to mail you cards, picture postcards of New York, in the return envelope that you send. So they do, and when you get those cards, you write your mother one, what a swell place it is, New York. Then you say you're all right and please don't worry about you, you'll write her more later. So then you send that in an envelope, to the same newsstand, with a note: 'Please mail the enclosed card for me.' So they do and that's that. Your mother thinks you're up there, she has no reason to worry, she don't call the cops or take any ad in that magazine. . . . Hey, Mandy, I try to help."

". . . OK, I guess that'll do it."

But in the night I kept thinking about it, and in the

morning I said, "Rick, getting back to Mother, who you may be getting sick of, but I can't get her out of my mind, and that idea you had, the card I'd mail from New York. It's OK, except for one thing: it'll take at lease a week, and this is Thursday, after me leaving home on Monday. Or in other words, sending a card *that* way, it'll be ten days from the time I took off, and in that time God only knows what she does from worry about me. And if we lost out for that reason, we'd just have ourselves to thank for not getting with it and..."

"OK, I've changed my mind. Call her."

"Oh, Rick, thanks, thanks, thanks."

"But not from here, not from the hotel. It's small, not like the one in Baltimore, and the girl on the board *could* get nosy, she *could* listen in. There's a drugstore down the street, next door to that restaurant we ate in last night, and all drugstores have a booth. Put in a station-to-station call, dial the area code, then your house number, and drop in the money, in coins, soon as the operator tells you. Then she won't know."

"OK, I'll do it now."

"But let's pack and check out. I'll wait in the lobby."

"Yes, that's the best way. *I'll* do it."

So I packed and went down, and he checked us out. Then he sat down to wait, and I said, "I'll make it as quick as I can, and then we can have breakfast. In the bus terminal would be nice."

"OK, I'll be right here."

I went out and walked down the street and, sure enough, there was the drugstore. I went in and changed five dollars into quarters, nickels, and dimes. Then I went in the booth and dialed. But I kept getting a busy. That was Mother, it turned out, calling the dispatcher downtown of Steve's trucking company to say he couldn't drive that day for reasons I'll get to later. Then she had to call his replacement, guy name of Jim Dolan, to tell him he had to drive—take the Parcel Post up to New York, then pick up wine off the boats, off the French Line boats at their pier, and bring it back on the down trip next day. So it kept her on the phone, and that's why I couldn't get through. I guess it went on for twenty minutes, until the fourth or fifth time that I tried, and then at last Mother came on. I said, "Mother, this is Mandy."

"... Well! Where are you? And what have you been up to?"

"Mother, is that how you talk to me? When I call with love in my heart? To explain to you what I did. I mean leaving home that way and leaving that note for you."

"I asked what you've been up to."

"Who says I've been up to anything?"

"You must have been. What about that coat?"

"... What coat?"

Because I own up that caught me completely off guard, and I had to stall, to get my mind together. She said, "The one you showed Ed Vernick!"

"How do you know about that?"

"He called me, that's how I know. To warn me that something went on—and put himself on notice. He did *not* mean to be dragged in. I ask you once more, where did you get it?"

"... From a store is where, a Baltimore store."

"You mean you stole it?"

"I mean I bought it."

"With what?"

"Money, what do you think?"

"Yes, but where did you get it?"

". . . I found it. On the floor of a car."

"What car?"

"I don't care to say what car!"

"The whole thing sounds like what Ed Vernick said, a mess. And you're not telling the truth about where you got that money! I don't believe you found it, on the floor of a car or anywhere. Mandy, if some man gave it to you, you're going to pay a price, you're going to pay one awful price, I warn you. Mandy, while you can, I beg you come home. It's only . . ."

"Mother, I can't. I won't."

"Where are you?"

"That I prefer not to say."

"Mandy, I have to know!"

"Mother, I promised not to say."

"Promised whom?"

"It's none of your business whom."

She began hooking it up then, with loud, snuffly sobs, about all she'd done for me, giving me "money, clothes, everything," and what a pest I'd been, "since the day you were born, bringing me nothing but grief." And then, "taking off that way, and leaving me that note. I never read such a thing in my life. And on top of that, going to see Ed Vernick and flaunting a mink coat at him. What on earth possessed you?"

"Mother, cool it."

". . . You dare say such a thing to me?"

"I do. Cool it. Knock it off!"

For some moments she didn't speak, and then in a different, more sensible tone she asked me, "Where are you?"

"I said I prefer not to say."

"But I have to know, there's a reason."

"What reason?"

"One I may have, but don't yet have."

"Where I am doesn't matter, as I'm traveling and first I stop one place, then another. When I'm settled I'll let you know."

"Then don't say you weren't told."

"Told what, Mother?"

"The . . . reason I'll have for wanting to know where you are. Which I'm not sure of yet but may be sure of later."

"Then, OK, Mother, I called up to say I'm all right, that you don't have to turn me in as a missing person or something, and . . . *have* you, by the way?"

"No! And after what Ed Vernick told me . . ."

"Then, don't. I'm OK."

"And that's all you have to say?"

"That's right. What do *you* have to say?"

". . . That you have all my love."

"And, Mother, you have mine."

Suddenly, both of us were crying, but with love mixed in, and then she kept saying, "My love and my prayers, I keep saying them over and over."

"Then, OK, Mother."

"OK . . . OK."

Then we'd both hung up, and I was standing there

in the booth, with an empty, queer feeling, the tears still on my cheeks.

Walking back to the hotel I kept thinking of Rick, how glad I'd be to see him, to be with him, to have him pat my hand and start talking about our island. But in the lobby he wasn't there. I looked in the dining room, remembering I'd been gone for some time and thinking he might have decided to eat breakfast. But he wasn't there, and I came back and went to the desk. I asked, "Would you have Mr. Ruth paged? Mr. Richard Ruth, please."

"Mr. Ruth has checked out. He left."

"He has *what*?"

"Checked out. Are you Mrs. Ruth?"

"Yes, I am. Did he leave a message for me?"

"No, Miss. He left this."

From behind the counter the clerk lifted my suitcase and set it on the desk in front of me. He kept staring in kind of a funny way. I said, "Oh, I see. Thanks."

"Yes, Miss."

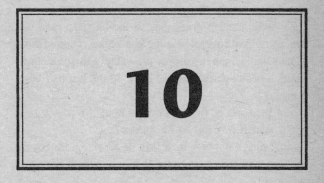

10

I took the suitcase, but a bellboy grabbed for it, and also for the coat, which I was carrying now, as it was warmer in Savannah than it had been in Baltimore. But I hung on to them both and staggered to a chair, where I sat down real quick, as I had to. I mean I was stunned and might have toppled if I tried to stay on my feet. Because, of course, I knew by now that Rick had played me a trick, sending me down to that drugstore so he could give me the air and skip with all that money. But the jolt wasn't all. I was hurt too, as at last I'd fallen for him, so I felt warm and close and friendly. On account of all that I sat there quite a few minutes, while the bellboy still stood by and the desk clerk studied me, like wondering what to do in case I became a problem, which I easily could have, as I had no idea what to do next. However, the first thing seemed to be to get on the trail of Rick. So at last I motioned the bellboy and let him take the bag and load me into a cab. I tipped him and told the driver, take me to the bus terminal.

At the terminal I paid him and went inside and at that hour, which was no more than a quarter to nine, there wasn't much going on, so the baggage man was sitting on his counter reading the paper. I asked him, "Did a young man in a zipper jacket and gabardine slacks claim a heavy black suitcase here? In the last half hour, I mean?"

"Yeah, about twenty minutes ago."

"Which way did he go, please?"

"I didn't notice which way he went. . . . Hey, wait, so happens I did. Last I saw of him he was at the ticket window."

"Thanks. Thanks ever so much."

I asked the man at the ticket window, "A young man in zipper coat, gabardine slacks, and long dark hair: do you remember what ticket he bought? Maybe twenty minutes ago?"

"Miss, I don't take note of their coat, their pants, or their hair. All I see is their money. No, I don't remember."

I went out on the platform, where people get on the buses, and, of course he wasn't there. I asked a man in uniform which buses had left in the last twenty minutes, and he said, "Atlanta local; Memphis express."

"Thank you so much."

I went to the taxi stand and there was my cab where I'd left it. I got in and told the driver, "Police station, please."

"OK. . . . Something wrong, Miss?"

"I want to report a theft."

"Police station's where you do it."

But then, after two or three blocks I panicked; I was so terrified. I realized what it would mean, that I would be questioned and would have to tell it all, not only about the money but also about the coat, so I'd have to give it up. I said, "I've changed my mind. I don't want the police station yet. I must find a place to stay, so I'll be settled down before I do anything. Where can I go, do you know?"

"You mean like to a motel?"

"I doubt if they'd take me in."

"They don't like young girls, that's right."

"I have to go somewhere, though."

"How about to the Y? They might take you in."

"I don't know much about them."

"Oh, they will take you in, of course. That is if you can pay? You got money, Miss?"

"I have some, yes."

"Be around five dollars a night."

"I can afford that much."

"Maybe a little bit more now. Say, this inflation really hurts. Everything's going up—except us. We have to charge the same."

"Y's fine. Take me there, please."

So we were passing a park, one of dozens they have in Savannah, and he drove around it so we were headed back the way we had come. And I began thinking of how I'd have to buy a paper for the want ads it would have, and I would begin, where I left off in Baltimore, trying to find a job. And then all of a sudden I up-chucked—not really, not the way Rick wanted to do, to make a mess there in the cab. I mean in my mind, so everything came up. It all came up in a flash, what Rick had done to me, how rotten it was, and how I refused to take it, lying down, sitting down, or any other way. I said to the driver, "I'm sorry, I've changed my mind again. Back to the bus terminal, please."

"The terminal it is."

I knew what I had to do.

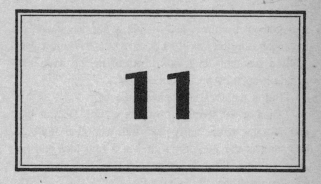

11

I got to Washington around ten o'clock and, instead of taking the bus out, went all the way by cab, as I was pretty tired by then and wanted to get there. So it was $4.25, and I gave the driver five dollars. Then I went up to the front porch, walking on the grass so my footsteps wouldn't be heard. I peeped in the front window and couldn't see anything, but a light was on in the living room, so I knew somebody was home. I let myself in with my key, making as little noise as I could, and then from the hall saw Steve asleep in the chair by the arch, the one to the dining room. He was all sprawled out, his necktie pulled to one side, his shirt open at the throat, his belt unbuckled, and his pants half unzipped, while beside the chair on the floor were six or eight beer cans standing around. I set the bag down, opened the closet and hung up the coat, then went in the living room and sat down in the chair by the door. Everything looked the same, the furniture a little bit scuffed, the rug with rose border, the aquarelles of Venice, and the color TV by the fireplace. It came to me about Steve, that if he was more or less drunk he might start something with me, so I got out a knife I had bought at the newsstand in Savannah. On the box it said "BOY SCOUT," but it was really a switchblade. I took it out of my handbag and sprung it open by pressing the button.

But at the *click* he opened his eyes.

Then he sat staring at me like a goof. He was big and thickset, maybe thirty years old, with kind of a bull look, but at the same time kind of a frog look. So he stared for some little time, then rubbed his eyes and stared some more. Then: "Mandy, is that you?"

"Well, who do you think it is?"

"I mean are you really there?"

"I think so, yes."

"Can I come over and touch you?"

But at that I picked up the knife and warned him, "I don't mind being touched, but if you start something with me, you're getting this in the gut. Did you hear what I said, Steve? I bought it special for you, and you make one pass out of line, I'm letting you have it."

"I won't do anything to you."

"Well, see that you don't."

So he came over and touched me with his finger, poking me on the shoulder, like he thought I might vanish or something. I said, "And another thing, Steve, you smell to high heaven of beer. So don't come any closer, please. I just don't care for beer, 'specially stale beer that makes me sick."

"I'll fix that right away."

Then his pants started to slide, and he grabbed them and zipped them up, then fastened his belt. Then he went over and picked up the cans, piling them in his arms, and went through the arch to the dining room and on through to the kitchen. Then pretty soon he was back, with his shirt buttoned, his necktie pulled up, and his hair combed back neat. That way he looked kind of nice, and I thanked him for showing respect. "And the stink is gone, I hope. I rinched my mouth out, rinched it out good, with Listerine."

He came close, and I said, "That's better."

"Mandy, I've been through the fires. When you left and I came home the next day and then your mother showed me your note, I thought I would die. I thought I would and didn't care if I did. I didn't want to live anymore. And then, after what happened today, the roof fell in—it's why I started in on the beer. You have to admit, it's not any weakness of mine, but I'd come to the end of the plank. Well? I'm not any drunk, am I?"

"OK, if it makes you feel better."

"Then I opened my eyes, and there you were."

"But what happened today?"

"It's like the sun came up. And the moon."

"I asked you what happened today."

"All in due time, I'll tell you."

"It's due time now. Where's Mother?"

"She's . . . not here."

"Her car's in the garage, though."

"That's right. She left it."

"Well, Steve, say something! Where is she?"

". . . She got married."

"She what?"

"Got married. To that guy, the one she's been stepping out with. Mandy, you have to know about him!"

"You mean that Wilmer? The one that has the distillery?"

"Yeah, him."

"But how could she, being married to you?"

". . . Almost married to me. Mandy, we were going to have it done, soon as she got straightened out on that thing with Vernick. But he stood in the way, and then when he wanted to get married again himself, he stood aside and that unblocked it. So she sued and that was that. But by that time she was suspicioning me, and we never did get around to it. She was free to marry any time she pleased."

"Suspicioning you of what?"

"Mandy, you have to know."

"Something having to do with me?"

"You've been my life for a long time."

"Is that when she moved to her room?"

"Yes, that's when . . . but by that time Wilmer had showed again, after bumping into her by accident on the street in Washington one day. So they started up again. But before she could marry him, she had to arrange about you—that's what she called it, 'arrange,' when she sat down and talked to me today while waiting for him. And she admitted she had hoped you would fall for me, marry me, and . . ."

"Well, I won't!"

"OK, but don't leave me, Mandy. I can stand anything but that! Not again!"

"You mean I just stay here with you?"

"I'll behave, I promise you. But listen, you did love me once! I could feel it. I can't be mistaken!"

"As my father! When I thought you were!"

"OK. Let me be him again!"

"Steve! It's all I've been looking for!"

"Oh, Mandy, it would make me so happy!"

"Then, I'll think about it."

He backtracked then, to tell more, and I kind of put things together: how Mother had held off her marriage until I was out of the way, and how this morning, when she thought I was, the idea popped in her mind that she'd have a showdown about it, and then if the answer was yes, she'd call me back and tell me—but I wouldn't say where I was. So it seemed the answer came pretty quick, that Mr. Wilmer not only told her yes but to stand by and he'd be right down, which he was in a couple of hours. So they went to Dover, Delaware, where there's no waiting period, and then called Steve from there—and how he celebrated was to get himself slopped on beer. Before they left she brought Mr. Wilmer in, "the first time I'd met him, Mandy. A real nice guy, a big shot as you know right away, just by looking at him." And while waiting for him she talked, "the first time in her life she ever leveled with me, to tell it like it was, friendly and straight and honest." Then he got back to me and came to where I was, in the chair, and touched me, my cheek, hair, and knee; I still had on the hot pants I'd put on in the room at Savannah. Then he took my hand and kissed it. So then I patted him and felt like I had before, when I'd climb all over him and muss him and punch him and tickle him. Then at last I said, "OK, Steve, be my father."

He kissed me then, on the forehead.

I said, "You mind if I fix myself something? I didn't have any breakfast and didn't get off anywhere. Off the bus, I mean, to eat."

"You mean you haven't eaten all day?"

"Or drunk anything either. I feel kind of funny."

"Well, there's eggs out there, of course, and bacon and stuff, but you're not fixing yourself anything. You're going out, and I'm taking you. That Bladensburg place is still open."

So we went to the place in Bladensburg, which is a bar that also serves food, and he ordered me steak, fried potatoes, and slaw, with pie a la mode for dessert, and had the same himself, as he hadn't eaten either. So everything was good, and right away I commenced feeling better. But it was cool and I'd put on the coat, and he kept staring at it. At last he asked, "Mandy, is that the coat? That Vernick called about?"

"Oh? She told you about that, then?"

"I was half the night calming her down."

"She was still kind of upset, talking to me."

"Where did you get it, Mandy?"

"Is that any business of yours?"

"I hope to tell you it is. Because if a guy gave it to you, I know what he got in return. I ask you once more, where did you get that coat?"

He got the same wild look in his eye he always used to get when he took down my panties and beat me, and I took out the knife once more. I snapped it open and held it in front of me. I said, "Suppose a guy did? Suppose he did give it to me? Suppose he got what you think? What then?"

He clasped his hands together, and I could see the knuckles whiten. Then he closed his eyes. Then after a long time: "OK, I take back what I asked. It's none of my business where you got the coat."

"You're not taking my panties down?"

"Well, not here, I hope."

He laughed but right away caught a sob before it came out, kind of gulped it back, in a way that left me shook. I mean all of a sudden he didn't look like a bull, or even like a frog, but a guy with a round face, a nice guy that I liked very much. I felt warm toward him and reached out my hand, first putting the knife away. I patted his hand and told him, "No guy gave it to me."

"For that piece of news, thanks."

"I did run off with one, that much is true, that I met at the bus stop, and I meant to do something with him, I can't pretend I did not, to get even with you for beating me up, and a little bit at Mother for letting you. I would have but he couldn't."

"What do you mean he couldn't?"

"He was scared."

"What of?"

"Everything. Me, maybe. The cops."

"Why them?"

"We helped out on a holdup."

"You helped out on a . . . what did you say?"

"Holdup. Of a bank."

"What bank?"

"Chesapeake Banking and Trust. In Baltimore."

But if it had been in the Washington papers, he hadn't paid any attention and hadn't caught it on TV. I mean he'd never heard of our holdup, and I had to tell him about it, which I did, beginning with how we'd been propositioned, Rick and I, by that pair there at the bus stop, what happened inside the bank, how I drove the getaway car, and how we went from one place to the other. Then I told how we got to Savannah and how Rick had sent me out to call Mother. Then I told about coming back, only to find I'd been given a stand-up so he could skip with the money. By then it was boiling out of me, and I was so mad I could hardly see. I said, "Steve, if it's murder they charge Rick with, on account of that guard being killed, and if he gets the gas chamber, that's perfectly all right with me. I want him caught and given the works! That money's half mine! Do you hear? It's half mine! It's..."

But he jumped up and put his hand on my mouth, as people were turning around and commencing to stare. He said, "You done, Mandy? You finished with your supper? Come on, we're going home!"

So he paid and tipped real quick, and we went out and got in his car. But going home I kept it up, getting slightly wild and always coming back to it: "That money is half mine! How dare he do that to me?" When we got home I was still hooking it up, but soon as we were inside he put his arms around me, kissed me, and patted me quiet, then said, "Mandy! It's not even a little bit yours! It belongs to the bank. Can't you understand that? The bank and the bank's depositors!"

"But nobody knows it was us!"

"Mandy, it's not what they know; it's what's right!

And what the law is! And what's going to happen once the truth begins to come out."

"OK, but I want him caught!"

"Sit down, let me think."

So we sat on the sofa, he holding on to my hand while he tried to figure out what he was going to do. Pretty soon he said, "I have to call your mother."

"Why do you?"

"To head her off from going away. *And* to try and get Wilmer in—put the bite on him if I can. He's a big shot, Mandy, and that's what this needs, first of all."

"Where is Mother? Where are they?"

"At his home, I would assume."

"You mean where the distillery is?"

"That's right. Rocky Ridge, in Frederick County."

He told a little more about what had happened that morning: Mother's call to Mr. Wilmer, after she talked to me, and her letting him have it straight: put up or shut up, now that I was out of the way. So he put up, quick. But, as Steve went on to say, "He must have been caught by surprise, with stuff hanging fire up there, so he'd have to go back for a while, at least for one night it would seem, before taking off tomorrow for the Riviera, like she said they were going to do in that call she put in from Dover. To me, I mean. She called to say it was done, that they were married, so good-bye, good luck, and God bless."

"Then, they must be up there."

So he sat down by the phone in the hall, got the number from information, and called. Then: "Sal?" But even from where I sat I could hear how furious she was from the way she yelped. I couldn't hear what was said but the sound of her voice came through, and it was just like glass—glass screeching on glass. He let her run down, then said, "Yes, Sal, I know what night it is, but you don't, I'm sorry to say. At least not the other half of the night, which is what I'm calling about. To you it's your wedding night. To me it's the night Mandy came home, and that means you're not going away tomorrow. You're not going anywhere, Sal. She's in terrible trouble, and you have to stand by. Do you hear me? *You have to*—until it's cleared up, if it's ever cleared up." All that got was more screaming, but he cut her off quick. He asked, "Is Mr. Wilmer there? Will you let me speak to him?"

Then: "Mr. Wilmer?"

Things quieted down then, as two guys talked to each other, deciding what should be done. Turned out Mr. Wilmer knew about the holdup from reading the *Baltimore Sun* instead of the Washington papers, and took an even more serious view of it than Steve did, if that was possible. Finally Steve wound up, "OK, then, Mr. Wilmer, I'll hold everything till you get here. I'm sorry, I hated to call, this night of nights, but I had to. I didn't have any choice. Because, frankly, I'm not sure I could swing it myself, what has to be done about Mandy. And you being in with all kinds of big wheels, especially lawyers. OK, I'll knock it off till you get here . . . Yes, she's here."

I took the phone then, calling him "Mr. Wilmer," and he was awful nice. He said, "Mandy, I'm your new father."

"Steve is my father now."

"OK, then, I'm your mother's new husband."

"Then, pleased to meet you."

"Mandy, all I want to say is, you have a friend."

"Thank you, Mr. Wilmer."

"But who is this 'Mr. Wilmer'?"

"I try to show respect."

"Your mother wants to talk to you."

So then Mother came on, and I don't put in what she said, as this is no time to repeat it. I mean she was bitter, bawling me out for cutting her out of her trip to Europe, "which I've looked forward to all my life and now have to give up." But as Steve said, when at last she hung up, "That's your mother all over. All she thinks about, all she ever thought about, is having a good time. Where's the Riviera? This place she was going to?"

"Somewhere in France, I think."

"Swinger's heaven, wherever it is."

When we were back on the sofa in the living room, Steve said they'd be down in the morning, as soon as they could make it. He said, "The main thing is Mr. Wilmer has a lawyer, a big wheel in Baltimore, who doesn't take this kind of case as a general rule but when he does is the best in the business."

I said, "But what's all the excitement about? If I turn Rick in, which I'm certainly going to do, I get munity, don't I?"

"*Imm*unity."

"Immunity, then."

"You do *if* you do."

"What's that supposed to mean?"

"There's no certainty to it. That's what scared him so. Mr. Wilmer, I mean. In Baltimore, on account of that guard being dead and the papers blasting off that something has to be done, he's not sure about anything—whether immunity will be granted or clemency consented to or any of the things that in some other case, with no death being involved, might be possible."

"Don't they want their money back?"

"That's our big chance."

So then it was time to go to bed, and I wasn't at all sure how Steve was going to act, our first night alone in the house. I went to my room, undressed, brushed my teeth, did my hair, put my pajamas on, and went to bed. I had my own bathroom, so that much presented no problem. But then, when my light was turned out, here came the tap on my door. I thought to myself, "This is it. Now I'll find out where I'm at." I tried to tell myself I wasn't going to mind, that there had to be a first time and it might as well be with Steve. Just the same, I felt pretty sick as I called, "Come in."

He came.

He bent over and kissed me on the forehead. Then he whispered, "Good night, little Mandy."

"Good night, Steve."

"You see, I keep my promises."

"For that I thank you, Steve."

He sat on the bed and went on, "Mandy, there's something I want to explain . . . why I paddy-whacked you."

"Steve, you beat me up."

"OK, call it that."

"I call it what it was."

"It was not for the reason you said, the one that you screamed at me more than once while I held you across my knee. To feel your bottom, you said. It wasn't that at all. It was because I thought you were stepping out with that bunch Amy Schultz runs around with, and it almost set me crazy. Mandy, I couldn't take it. Talking with her, after you left, trying to get on your trail, your mother found out that you weren't . . . for that, and this other thing that you told me, that nothing went on on this trip between you and that boy you ran off with. I can stand all the rest and not mind. I can even glory in you, the nerve that you showed that day to hold steady there at the wheel of the car they put you to drive and get out of there with the money and the boy. Mandy, you couldn't do wrong for me. It's what I've been wanting to say."

He got up then and kissed me once more on the forehead, but I pulled him to me, held him close, and kissed him on the mouth. I said, "Steve, now I know you're my father. I love you."

"Little Mandy, good night."

Then he tiptoed to the door, and as he went out we waved to each other and laughed.

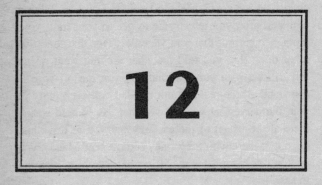

12

We were both up early, and I put on the blue dress, the one I'd left home in, and combed out my hair, and put a blue ribbon around it. Soon as I'd made us some breakfast we began straightening up to kind of get things in order. Then I put on an apron to go out front and sweep off, as we had two cedar trees and that time of year they shed, so brown fuzz was all over the place, 'specially the walk. So then Mrs. Minot was there, the woman who lived next door. She wanted to know where I'd been, and I said, "Oh, I come and go. First I'm here, and then I'm not here." Then she asked where Mother was, and I said she'd be here directly. She said, "She left yesterday with a man, in a car, and three bags that he carried out. Has she gone away again?" So, of course, what she really meant was, not only about Mother but about me, had I spent the night alone in the house with Steve? I looked at her straight and asked, "Mrs. Minot, do you know what curiosity did to the cat?" And when she didn't answer I said, "It killed her, that's what. And I really and truly hope it does not do the same to you." So on that there was nothing much she could do but go in her house again, which she did.

"What was that about?" asked Steve when I went in again.

"Woman sticking her nose in our business and getting it cut off is all."

"She's done nothing but try to find out about you."

"What she found out wouldn't choke a gnat."

I got out the vac, but he said, "Mandy, put it back and put that broom away. The house is OK like it is. Your mother's seen it worse. We're in for one God-awful day, so let's not throw it away working for Mr. Hoover. Let's take it easy till they get here."

So I put the things away and we sat in the living room, trying to take it easy. We did, I guess, for ten minutes, just sitting and not saying much. But then I had to talk. I said, "This Vernick now? Why did he say what he did, that I wasn't his child?"

"I don't exactly know."

"'Don't exactly' means you do. So, why?"

"Mandy, it's none of my business."

"But it's my business, Steve. That means it better be yours, 'less you want me to leave you again."

He got up, went to the window, and stood looking out. He stood there a long time, and I knew he was hoping they'd come. But it was only a quarter to ten, and they didn't. I repeated it one more time: why did Vernick say what he did? And then at last he said, "OK, if you insist, I'll tell you what I heard, what I've picked up from time to time, what may be true or may not be. Did you hear what I said? It may be true or may not be. But this much I'll guarantee: when I've told it you'll wish I hadn't. Because I loved your mother once and think I understand her. I can defend what she did, take the side of a fourteen-year-old, a pretty teenage girl who liked a good time, who *lived* for a good time then, later, and now. It's OK with me what she did. I'm not so sure it will be with you."

"Listen, *I have to know*!"

"Then: she was playing around with Vernick."

"That I can't understand! It's weird!"

"But not like robbing a bank."

"OK, OK."

"She was fourteen years old. Teenagers *are* weird."

"I said OK. She was playing around with Vernick."

"And then kind of ran into trouble."

"You mean she came up pregnant?"

"Yes, except she wasn't quite sure yet. She was just a kid and kept hoping and hoping and hoping ... and waiting. She was afraid to tell her mother. And then at last she'd waited too long. She had to go in a home and have the child, have you. Then she put the bite on Vernick, and his father backed her up, made him marry her. That was a week before you arrived, and his father, still wanting to do the right thing, went to her father, your grandfather Gorsuch, to pay what the home had cost. But he said, Mr. Gorsuch did, that he hadn't yet got the bill, but whatever it was there was no hurry about it. But Vernick's father wanted to lean over backwards and, instead of waiting, went himself to the home to give them a check so no bill would be sent Mr. Gorsuch. But the woman couldn't say, or wouldn't say, how much the bill would be, and he thought it was pretty funny. He asked her to please find out. And when she stepped in the next office, he tiptoed over to listen. And what he heard stood his world on its head, and his son's world, and your mother's world, and your world."

"What did he hear?"

"*'But that's all been taken care of!'* "

"Taken care of? By whom?"

"That's what stood all those worlds on their heads."

"Steve, I asked you, by whom?"

"I don't know by whom!"

After a long time I asked, "Does Mother know?"

"I can't say what she knows." And then: "Mandy, she was a teenage girl, a kid that liked a good time. Who knows what she knows?"

"But if she doesn't know, I don't!"

"I said, if I tell it you'll wish I hadn't."

"And I don't have any father!"

"You have me . . . if you want me."

"Want you? *Want you?* Steve, I want you as I've never wanted anything! Steve, be my father! Be my father always. I've . . . I've been hit by too many trucks. I can't take any more!"

By that time I was crying, and he came over and patted me, taking me in his arms and kneeling beside my chair. He said, "Mandy, I knew it would hurt. I warned you it was going to. I begged you not to make me tell it. But a deal is a deal, and if that's what you wanted I had to go through. I want to be your father, and I promise never to take advantage. Well? I proved that I wouldn't, didn't I? Last night?"

"Yes, Steve, and I was so happy."

"There's one other thing, little Mandy."

"Yes, Steve? What is it?"

"You can count on me, all the way."

He knelt there some little time, patting me, kissing me, and calming me down. Then we got to laughing, when he got his handkerchief out and let me blow my nose. He said I sounded "like the B&O freight every night blowing for College Park." Laughing was what I needed, I guess, and I began to feel a lot better. And then when I looked there was Mother, skipping up on the porch in that graceful way she had. Steve jumped up and scrambled out in the hall, opening the door for her. Then she was in, pulling his ear and kissing him, I guess from habit, or maybe forgetting who she was married to. She was all smiles for him but hadn't any for me. I mean she had hazel eyes, which took up the green she always wore, to contrast with her hair, which was a beautiful dark red. And they could be warm and friendly and gay, and in fact usually were, 'specially for a man. They flashed that way for Steve, but when she saw me they got hard, and when they were hard they were hard. I mean like a couple of marbles. Then she started in letting me have it, taking up right where she left off on the phone the night before. She ran over it, what a pest I had been since the day I was born. She was 'specially bitter about Vernick, about my going to him.

But I cut in on her and asked, "Speaking of him, why would he say what he did? That I wasn't his child at all?"

"To save himself money is why! He owes me nine

thousand six hundred and fifty dollars of the fifty-a-month I was given that the court awarded me for your support, of which he's never paid me one cent! That's why he pretends you're not his. But you are, just the same. And a chip off the old block, I would say. My, how your character resembles his!"

So, of course, that made me feel fine, but she went right on, feeling sorry for herself, "And here now at last, when I thought I might have some peace, a change, a chance to relax, perhaps enjoy myself a little, you have to do this to me!"

But on that Steve got in it. He said, "Sal, maybe to you it's just an interrupted good time, but to her, to Mandy, it could mean going to prison, years out of her life, and *perhaps* even worse. So knock it off about your trip. We got real things to worry about."

"My, my, my! Listen at him!"

She went over and popped a kiss on his cheek, which for some reason 'furiated me. I said, "Whatever the truth about me, between you and this awful rat Vernick, this much seems to be clear, which nobody can deny: last night, Mrs. Wilmer, was the first night in your life that you had the connubial bliss while united in holy wedlock. So I can well understand that you hated to be interrupted by such a crumb as me. Is that what you call it, connubial? Like in nubial? Which means hot in the pants but light in the head?"

That settled her hash but good. She gave a yelp, staggered to the sofa, stretched herself out, and bawled. But even during that all I could really think of wasn't how I had clobbered her but how pretty she was. She was still a month less than thirty and just about my size,

medium verging on small. Her face was good-looking
all right, but slightly beat-up, so it seemed. I don't mean
from somebody banging it, but from banging on the
inside, like she didn't sleep good at night. Her eyes, like
I said, were hazel, with a friendly, flirty expression,
'specially for men when she looked at them, but at the
same time had kind of a hunted expression, like she
wasn't quite sure of the look she'd get in return. Her
hair was something to see, dark glossy red, and she
combed it out on her shoulders in big, thick curls. But
the main thing about her, what you couldn't take your
eyes off of, was her figure. It was slim and soft and
willowy, about my size. And did she know how to dress
it! Today she had on a bottle-green linen suit to go with
her hair in contrast, the skirt short as the law allowed to
show off her beautiful legs. She was something to see
all right, doing her stagger, but not any stumpy stagger
like she was going to fall. It was a slow, sad, and slinky
stagger, kind of sexy if you know what I mean, much
like her regular walk, except not with the bottom twitch.
When she finally got to the sofa, she didn't flop down
kerbam. She kind of melted down till she was all stretched
out, one toe touching the floor in a graceful way, the
back of her skirt hiked up to show her good-looking
bottom. Then, one sob at a time, she commenced doing
her stuff, till she was bawling good, with Steve still there
saying nothing, and me hollering at her, saying over again
what I had said, till he cut me off with a wave of one
hand.

That's when the bell rang and Steve let in Mr. Wilmer, who had been gassing the Caddy up. He waved at
me from the hall, and I have to say I was impressed.

He's a blond guy, not much older than Mother, though two or three years I would say, with light curly hair and a nice clean, well-scrubbed look. He's big and had on a gray summer suit, but with a collar that hugged his neck and a cut like in the ads. He stood there and smiled when I waved back at him. But then came a whoop from Mother, and he stepped into the room and saw her. Real quick he went over and knelt, taking her in his arms and whispering stuff to her. Then she really hooked it up, "Ben, I can't help it, I have to! It's not it, it's her, that dreadful little viper!"

"That *what*?"

"Viper!" I screamed. "It means rattlesnake . . . and shows what she thinks of me, exactly what she thinks!"

"Oh! I thought she said diaper."

"I had to shut her up," I said.

But at that, he came over to me, put his hand on my head, and asked, "Don't you know how to shut someone up? The quickest, surest way?" He waited and then went on, "You go over and give them a kiss. You cover their mouth with your mouth, and then they can't say anything. It shuts them up complete!"

"You think I would? With her?"

"I don't think. I know."

His voice was like ice, and Steve said, "You heard him, Mandy. Get going."

"I'll think about it."

But a big hand grabbed my wrist and yanked it, and then there I was beside Mother, my face being pushed against hers. So then I could taste her tears. So then I wanted to kiss her and did. And then, lo and behold, she kissed back, real hard, the first time in her life, in my life that she had. Then we were holding on to each other, crying and kissing and happy.

Pretty soon Mr. Wilmer lifted me up and led to a chair, where he pulled me down in his lap. Then he said, "OK, begin, Mandy. I have to know what happened." So I told it once more, like to Steve the night before, but maybe quicker this time, so it took no more than two minutes, call it five. When I finished, his face was screwed up like something was hurting him, and to make him feel better I said, "But no one suspicions us. No one has any idea. How could they? No one knows we were there!" But when I tried to go on, he laid his hand on my mouth and asked, "Can I borrow the phone?" And Steve took him to Mother's extension upstairs. He was back in a couple of minutes, saying, "I just talked to Jim Clawson, my lawyer, and it took a little persuading but he's agreed to take charge of the case. He may want a trial lawyer later, but as of now he's it. He wants us over there, at his office in Baltimore, at two o'clock, and as it's nearly eleven now, and we'll have to get some lunch, I'd say it's time we got started."

He said we could all go in his car, but Steve wanted me with him "so we each have our own transportation." I would have liked a ride in the Caddy but went with Steve as he said. But before Mr. Wilmer came down, and while we were waiting for him, Mother beckoned me over, made a place for me on the sofa, then pulled me down beside her and went back to kissing me. She said, "You're such a sweet, pretty thing, Mandy. I'd die before letting them harm you. You're my own, my won-

derful child. Now I feel it at last. Thanks to that wonderful man, my husband."

"*And* me," said Steve.

"And *you!*"

She got up and went over and kissed him.

13

Mr. Clawson was a guy around forty, in a blazer and gray slacks, tall and slim, but with square shoulders that looked pretty strong. He was the middle one of a firm, Digges, Clawson, and Llowndes, though I didn't meet the others, and he had offices in the Fidelity Building, which is big but pretty old, right in the center of town on Charles Street. It was only a couple of blocks from Marconi's, a nice place where we all four had lunch. And then we walked to the Fidelity Building, leaving the cars on the parking lot on West Saratoga Street, which was where the restaurant was. Mr. Clawson's office was one of a suite, with a reception room in front and a girl at a switchboard desk. The ceiling was high, with a mahogany desk, broadloom rug, leather chairs, and bookshelves to the ceiling lined with law books all in maroon. He sat us down very friendly, and after a few minutes' chat, with expressions of real surprise at the news of the wedding bells, he got down to brass tacks, and once more I had to tell it. But this time it took a lot longer because he kept questioning me about why Rick and I got in it. He kept talking about "coercion" and taking me over and over it, the effect it had on us, when Pal—or Matt Caskey, actually—kept tapping his gun. Then I saw he was heading me off from blaming the coat for it all, as I had when telling Steve and, of course, Mr. Wilmer too.

I owned up I was scared of the guns but insisted I wanted the coat to go and show my father; and that was the reason I had for telling those two guys yes. He seemed annoyed and studied me hard. Then pretty soon he said, "Mandy, the way you tell it, do you know who'll get immunity?"

"Me, I hope."

"Nobody. Do you know who, when the case comes to trial, is going to get acquitted? *The way you tell it*, I mean?"

"...I hadn't thought."

"Rick."

"Did you say *Rick*?"

"Yes. He was forced at gunpoint, to help out." He let that soak in and went on, "Do you know who's going to be convicted and sent to prison?"

"Well, I'm the only one left!"

"That's right, you."

It wasn't so much what he said as the hard, cold way he said it, and spite of all I started to cry. Mother came with a Kleenex and wiped my eyes. When she stepped aside he went on, "*As you tell it*, you went in of your own free will to get yourself a mink coat to flaunt in front of your father. Rick went in from having to, from being forced at gunpoint after doing his best to back out. That adds up to coercion."

"He stole the money, though!"

"He used it, *as you tell it*, as a shield from the bank guard's shots, after having once dropped it and started out to the car."

"I mean he stole it off *me*!"

"Mandy, quit being silly!"

That was Steve, cutting in to remind me we'd been over all that, when I started yelping at supper the money was half mine. He snapped, "How could he steal it off you when it wasn't even yours?" I guess I saw the point, but it still seemed to me that if no one knew we were in it, then it was ours, like finders-keepers. Mr. Clawson waited, then went on, "I've said, I've repeated, Mandy, *as you tell it*. So if you want Rick to go free while you spend ten years in prison, you keep on telling it that way. But if you want *immunity*, if on thinking it over you prefer it to serving time..."

"I don't think you like me very much."

"I like you fine. You're very easy to like, very pretty, very attractive. But I shouldn't deceive you just to get one of your smiles. That might be pleasant for me, but for you, in the Maryland Penitentiary, it might not be pleasant at all."

"It's not a question of liking."

Steve snapped it so sour that Mother had to make with the Kleenex again. Mr. Wilmer came over, touched my cheek, and whispered, "You're not doing very good."

"I know I'm not. I'm sorry."

But him being there made me feel better. He asked,

"Why don't you listen just once? 'Stead of giving an imitation of a bullhead calf?"

"OK."

Mr. Clawson laughed, so his face lit up real nice, and that helped. I said, "I tell it like it was."

"You mean you've been telling the truth?"

"Yes, sir."

"The whole truth might be more than you've told so far. As you tell it, and as I hear it, I can't believe that that gun had no effect. I have to believe it did, and that the coat notwithstanding, *it* was the main thing driving you into this crime. Still the gun I'm talking about. That's what I believe, after hearing you tell it. What about you, Mandy?"

"Well, of course I was scared of the gun, but..."

"Never mind the but for the moment. You were scared of the gun, first, last..."

"And during."

"That's it, now we're coming!"

"*I'd* have been paralyzed!"

That was Mother, turning her eyes on him so he responded with a smile, which no man ever denied her. He said, "So! We're getting somewhere at last, with no violation, not the slightest, of the truth. Next, of course, is the coat. Where is it, by the way?"

"I left it home."

Which I had, as the day was warm and a light jacket, which I had in my lap, was all that I'd brought with me. He said, "Fine, but before we go into it, what's to be told about it, there's one angle of this case that overshadows everything, and we have to go into it before we talk about coat, father, or anything else. I'm referring to Rick, of course."

"Oh, *him*!"

"You must join your case to his, do all in your power to help him."

"That yellow-bellied rat? Who ran out on me that way? Who played me that rotten trick?"

"It's precisely his yellow belly that's the key to the whole thing, the one chance you have to get off. Because in spite of the luck you both played in, in spite of your pad as it's called, this very nice room you were able to share, he was so scared he couldn't, and you didn't want him to. This couldn't have been invented; it's proof of the truth of your whole story any jury would have to believe: that both of you went along, took part in this dreadful crime from pure terror. And on top of that was Rick's perception of something you didn't see, his catching a sign that was passed that meant you both would be killed. All this, if you join your case with Rick's, *can* get you off. It *can* get you immunity, *can* extricate you from this mess. Once that approach is made, other things, like the coat, the reception you got from your father, your reasons for leaving home, pale into insignificance. You were a couple of panicky kids who did something you shouldn't have, but now, when at last you've thought it over, you're stringing with law and order, helping us recover the money, helping us find Rick, helping us show him that he must get with it too!"

"Mandy, I think that's it."

So said Mr. Wilmer.

"Of course it is."

So said Steve.

"But I hate him!"

So said I.

"Have you ever seen a prison?"

So said Mr. Clawson, and I started to cry again. But he was the one that time who took the Kleenex from Mother and wiped my tears with it. He went on, "I have, Mandy. I've had to go there once or twice in connection with legal matters. There's no such hell beyond the grave. There couldn't be, as no decent God would ever create what men have brought forth on this earth. It stinks. It hasn't one ounce of compassion from end to end, from top to bottom. No mouthful of decent food is ever served in it, no love is felt, no jokes are cracked, no hope ever shines in. And they keep you there years and years, so long it makes no sense, but you stay there just the same. Are you sure you hate that boy this much? That you'd go to prison to wreak revenge on him?"

"OK, I'll do what I can."

"You have to do better than that!"

"I'll fight for him, then."

"That's better."

"But I won't want to."

"Mandy, will you wake up?"

"Mr. Clawson, I'll really hit it a lick."

"That's what I want to hear. Kiss me."

I kissed him, and Mother started to cry. I started to cry. Mother gave him the Kleenex, but he wiped his own face off. Then we were laughing and pressing each other's hand.

* * *

Turned out, though, that beating some sense into my head was just the beginning of it. "Now," he went on, "we take up the next thing: who makes the pitch?"

"Break it down," said Mr. Wilmer, "so we know what you're talking about."

"Who faces the state's attorney for Baltimore City, or the assistant in charge of this case, the bank, and the police and pins them down to a deal—immunity for Mandy in return for what she knows, the help she'll be able to give in the recovery of the money."

"I thought that was your job, Jim."

"It would be my job, except that in this case it can't be. Because when I declare myself as her counsel, I have to surrender her or be charged with harboring a fugitive from justice. I can surrender her, that's true, clam her up under the Fifth Amendment, and to that extent freeze the game—stand pat and leave the next move up to them. The trouble is they will move, and so fast it'll take your breath. The second they know who she is, they'll get the rest one, two, three like that—Rick's identity, his whereabouts quite possibly, and anything else they need to get the money back and bring these kids to trial. Ethics bind me hand and foot. I can't make this pitch in the way it has to be made *if* we're to get anywhere, *if* we're to get a deal."

"Go on, Jim. What's the rest?"

"Someone must go to them, through me, of course, with news of a friend of his, sex as yet undisclosed; who helped out on that crime; who knows the police are off on a wrong scent trying to find the Rossi brothers; who is willing to help, with information that may be of value, in recovering that money; but who won't talk, won't say one word, one word of any kind, unless granted immunity."

"Meaning me?"

"Ben, meaning you as I would assume, *but* you're not involved in this crime, you can't take the Fifth Amendment, and as a material witness you can be made to talk."

"Yeah? How?"

"You can be jailed until you do."

"Now I have it."

He studied Mr. Clawson, trying to make up his mind whether to put his head on the block. He swears now he would have, and I believe him, but it didn't get that far. Suddenly Steve spoke up, "How about me, Mr. Clawson?"

"You? Mr. Baker, is that your name?"

"Yeah. And I'd go to jail for Mandy."

"You could stay there and stay there and stay there."

"If they *have* that much time."

"He'll do. This guy is elected."

Mr. Wilmer went over and took Steve by the hand. He said, "Steve, my hat's off to you." Mother went over and kissed him. I kissed him.

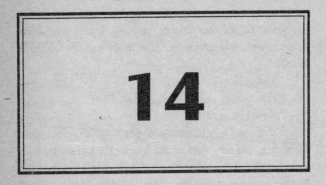

14

Next was to figure out how we would do to get the thing in the works, and Mr. Clawson said Steve should stay there, right in his office with him, while he called the state's attorney with his item of news. But while the discussion went on, he wanted me out of the way, as well as Mother and Mr. Wilmer, until the time would come for me to "do my stuff," as he put it. But at the same time he wanted me near, so I would be on call and get there quick when told. That way, he said, no time would be lost, "and we *could* wrap it up, right here, this afternoon." So Mr. Wilmer suggested a hotel, where we could be in a suite and at the same time be ready to come "as soon as we get your call and you give us the word." So lo and behold, we walked around the corner, Mother and Mr. Wilmer and I, to the same old hotel Rick and I had stopped at two nights before. Mr. Wilmer asked for sitting room, bedroom, and bath but, of course, had no luggage, as the car was still on the parking lot and he hadn't bothered to get it just to take us a block or two. So he took out his wallet to pay or show his credit card or whatever he meant to do, but the clerk held up his hand to stop him. He said, "Please, Mr. Wilmer! We don't have such rules for you."

What it means to be a big shot.

So the suite was even fancier than the room Rick and I had had, and as soon as the bellboy went Mother took off the green so it wouldn't get mussed and stretched out on the chaise lounge in her black pantyhose, black shoes, and black bra, like in *Playboy* magazine—'specially around the bra and what she had in it, which was plenty. Mr. Wilmer threw me a wink, and maybe I winked back, but I didn't take off my dress. Then he sat me down on the sofa and asked what was my favorite poem. I said, "The Rime of the Ancient Mariner."

"Really? Why?"

"It sends shivers down my back."

"You know it?"

"Some of it. Not all. It's awful long."

"Let's hear you recite what you know."

It seemed like a funny idea, but turned out he had a reason, as he later explained to me, which I'll tell all in due course, when I get to it. However, anything to please, and I commenced giving out. And he commenced watching me, not only listening but watching, as though he was seeing something about me that I didn't know about. When I came to the line "I shot the albatross," who got in it but Mother. "I'll say she did!" she popped off, and I'm telling you that broke it up. We all three got to laughing so I couldn't go on. So then, of course, we had kisses, and I had to kneel beside Mother to sniff her and touch her and feel how pretty she was. I said, "It's a mess from beginning to end, and I hate myself that I ever got into it. And yet it's almost been worth it, to bring me at last so close to my wonderful mother."

"Yes, Darling, and I've been thinking the same."

He sat on the edge of the chaise, holding one of her hands, while I kept kissing the other, and that's how we were when the phone rang. He answered, then said, "Steve's on his way up. Sally, get yourself dressed."

She took her time, as she always did, getting up from the chaise and sashaying into the bedroom, but at lease the door was closed when Steve sounded the buzzer. Mr. Wilmer let him in, and he burst out very excited, talking to both of us but looking mainly at me, "They're on their way over, Mr. Clawson, guy name of Haynes from the state's attorney's office, couple of detectives, a police stenographer, a guy from the bank and a guy from the insurance company. But, Mandy, I put it over. It's what I ducked out to tell you before they get here. They didn't want any piece of a deal, tried to break me, tried to make me spell it regardless, and, hey, they handled me rough. But Mr. Clawson kept looking at me, like trying to telegraph something, which he couldn't tell me about by whispering in my ear, as it would look like he was coaching me, which would have loused us, of course. Then at last I got it: no insurance man was there. *But*, the insurance company, of course, was the one under the boom. If the money was not recovered, they were the ones had to pay. So once I caught on to that, did I let them have it! I said, 'So you don't want money at all, just this person's blood, so you see justice done? My, how noble of you. I'm fainting from admiration.' Then I faced the guy from the bank, a vice president name of Clark, and cussed him out by the book. Then I said, 'Will you kindly stop being funny? You want me to name this person, that's Jake with me, but I do it to Mr. Big, not you. Get your bondsman in here! I won't spill it to nobody else! If he wants blood, OK, but could be he'd rather have dough.'

"I'd played the right card, I could feel it, and when I looked at Mr. Clawson, he had this smile on his face. The rest of it went fast. The insurance man was called and got there in just a few minutes, little guy name of Richter. And when he got the straight of it all, what he said to Clark made what I said sound like a Sunday school. He really went to town, telling him what he'd forgotten, that unless he took all possible steps to help in the money's recovery, 'your goddam bond is canceled.' And that did it. Mr. Clawson insisted they call a judge to get court approval by phone for immunity, but then at last the deal was made. That's when I slipped out, like to the little boy's room, to hightail it over here so I could tell you myself. Mandy, I did it. It was me."

I went over and kissed him. Mother had come in by then, in time to hear the last of it, and she patted him on the head. Mr. Wilmer gave him a wave of the hand. When the phone rang he took it and told us, "They're on their way up."

Real quick Steve said, "*Mandy?*"

"Yes, Steve?"

"Kind of put it on me. You know?"

But Mr. Wilmer said "Steve" real sharp.

"Yes sir?"

"Quit telling her what to say. It's up to her who she puts it on. She's in enough trouble already without any help from you."

"OK."

We sat down again on the sofa, me in the middle, Steve on one side, Mr. Wilmer on the other, each of them holding one of my hands. When the buzzer sounded Mother opened the door. She didn't look like *Playboy* anymore, but more like the *Ladies' Home Journal*, from being so elegant. And the black gloves topped it all off. They were cotton and elbow-length, but instead of wearing them she carried them, occasionally pulling them through one hand so she was oh, oh, oh, so casual, as though it was all of no real importance. And if you ask me, that helped. She let in quite a bunch, giving them each a separate smile, very friendly and warm: a bald-headed guy named Haynes, the assistant state's attorney in charge of the case; a woman in police uniform, carrying a stenotype case; two detectives, one carrying a tape recorder, the other cans of tape; a middle-aged man from the bank, introduced as Mr. Clark; a small, gray-haired man from Patapsco Mutual, introduced as Mr. Richter. And, of course, Mr. Clawson, who did the introducing.

So Mr. Haynes no sooner saw Steve than he commenced bawling him out "for giving me the slip," but Mr. Clawson cut him off. He said, "Jack, slipping over here first to help you out on this case is *not* giving you the slip! I suggest you quit hacking at him for what at worst was a breach of protocol, amounting to nothing.

So he should have asked your permission to leave. So OK. Let's get on."

"Then, I stand corrected."

He wasn't too nice about it, but it gave me quite a buzz that even a state's attorney would back down to Mr. Clawson. However, he kept on talking to Steve, "All right, Baker, where's the guy?"

"What guy, Mr. State's Attorney?"

"The one involved in this case?"

"I didn't say guy. I said person. Right here."

He held up my hand after kissing it, and Mr. Haynes stared, hardly able to speak. Then he said, "The . . . person? Is a girl? Is *that* girl?"

"That's right, Mr. Haynes. Just gives you a nice rough idea how wrong a tree it is that you've been barking up."

Mr. Haynes asked me, "What's your name?"

"Amanda Vernick, Mandy, they call me."

"Well, well, well!"

"I drove the getaway car."

He kept staring at me, but during that the phone rang, and Mr. Wilmer, after answering, told him, "It's for you."

He said hello and right away took a looseleaf notebook from his pocket and wrote in it with a ballpoint. He asked questions like "When was this?" and "What hotel?" and at last hung up. Turning back to us he said, "We could even say chasing my tail. They found Vanny Rossi in the Rogers Hotel on West Fayette Street dead from an overdose of heroin. But the checkout showed he'd been in that room for a week, without leaving it once. So it's clear: *He* didn't drive that car."

"I told you, sir. I did."

"Then you're a friend of Vito Rossi's?"

"No, sir, I don't know him."

"But he helped out in the bank. He held the basket the money was thrown in. The girl, the teller who handled it, picked him out from one of our mug shots."

"She made a mistake. The guy looked like Rick."

"Who's Rick?"

"The boy who *did* hold the basket."

"How do you know Vito Rossi looked like him?"

"From his picture, the one that was in the paper."

"Oh. Oh, that's right, so it was."

It was hard prying him loose from the idea the Rossis were in it, even with one of them dead, but at last Mr. Clawson said, "Jack, why don't you let her get on? Tell you what actually happened? I assure you, from even the little I know, she was there, she knows, and can clear the thing up in ten minutes. So far as the tree goes, your tail, and the false scent the police have been on, it's happened before and reflects no discredit on anyone, especially after that girl, from overeagerness to help, made her mistake on that picture. Mandy, if you'll let her, can clear everything up."

"OK, Mandy, start clearing."

They set it up then for me. I moved to one end of the sofa, with Mr. Haynes at the other, both with mikes on our chests and the tape recorder between. On the cocktail table in front of us the girl set her stenotype machine and sat on the floor beside it, so they had me two ways, on tape and on stenotype. Why, don't ask me, I don't know. The detectives, the bank man, and the insurance man all gathered around, some sitting, some standing, while Mother sat near me, holding my hand, on a chair by the sofa, while Steve and Mr. Wilmer stood by. Mr. Haynes said, "Mandy, will you give your name, age, and home address into the mike, and then go on in your own words and tell what happened Tuesday. What led to it and what it led to."

So I did, almost the way I'd already told it three times, to Steve, Mr. Wilmer, and that same day to Mr. Clawson, except that I left stuff out, though not to speak untruth. Like, on why I left home I said, "I was kind of fed up, like with school and A-square plus B-square, and decided to visit my father a while." That was all and everyone nodded, like A-square plus B-square would kind of feed anyone up. So, except for the algebra, I didn't put it on either one, Steve or Mother, I mean. And about my father I said, "I called him that night, but me shacking with Rick kind of loused it, my moving in with him." And about the mink coat I said, "I wanted it, wanted it bad, as I wanted my father to know I wasn't mooching off him." And about Pal and Bud I said, "Mr. Haynes, I don't know if you ever faced guns, but I tell you one thing: the butt of one sticking out, a blue butt in an armpit holster, is going to talk louder to you than anything you ever heard." And about Rick I said, "I bear him no ill will, but I'm sick and tired of this thing, and I want to help all I can to get it all the way cleared up and get that money back, as I think can be done if you handle it right with him, with Rick I'm talking about, so he cooperates. I'm doing him a favor, I feel, by telling it all like it was, so the word can go out to him, so he'll read in the papers about it and then go and give himself up, so he'll be shut of it too. So OK, Mr. Haynes, that's all. I've told it like it was, partly to wind the thing up, and partly for Rick's own sake."

"OK, Mandy, thanks."

In between it had come out about Mother's remarriage, which was mainly due, I said, "to this wonderful man, Mr. Wilmer, trying to make it up to her for her upset at losing me." They all kind of bowed very friendly, first to her, and then to Mr. Wilmer, a little extra for him, I thought, as he was a very big wheel. When I finished, the question of money came up, and I had to hand over the balance of what I had left in my handbag from what I had grabbed from the floor of the car, less what I'd spent on the coat, meals, and bus fare. Then the coat was brought up, and they decided an officer should "impound it," as Mr. Haynes said, as evidence, after going to Hyattsville. But then Mother got in it, protesting, "Evidence of *what*? It was part of the crime, but it is a beautiful thing, and to have it kicking around in some kind of locker under the tender care of *policemen*."

"Something wrong with them?" asked a detective.

"*Everything*, from a mink coat's point of view." Then, very snappish: "It's the woman's angle, of course, but I remind you, *it's her coat*."

"It was bought with stolen money."

"Just the same, it was bought!"

They had it some more, but then Mr. Clawson got in it. He said. "Jack, technically speaking, Mrs. Wilmer is right. It's not evidence of anything the indictment will cover, assuming we get that far. So far as the money goes, the money she found in the car that she used to pay for this coat, Ben Wilmer has already agreed to make good whatever it amounts to, which covers the coat and any turpitude it involves. If you want, we'll stipulate."

"For the time being, then, OK."

"It'll be there, don't worry, *in case*."

It was decided that I'd be released in Mother's custody, and then they all got up. Mr. Haynes told me, "OK, Mandy. The lady will type this up today, and then tomorrow you can come in to my office in City Hall and sign. Mr. Clawson will bring you over."

"Will do. And thanks, Jack, for being so decent."

They left to call the FBI and get them started looking for Rick, and to go on their teletype to police all over the country.

Then at last we were alone, Mother, Mr. Wilmer, Steve, and I, but Mother had barely started. She ran with real quick steps, her bottom all aquiver, to the phone and gave the girl a number. I felt my heart go bump, as I recognized it at once as Vernick's. A man's voice came on and she started to talk. She brought him up to date, telling how things stood, real quick, and went on, "Ed, Mandy handled it beautifully and really gave you a break. She said not one word about the rotten way you treated her or the things you alleged about me. They'll be calling you, especially the papers will, but I'm telling you, Ed, one crack from you out of line, and I'm letting you have it. You may have forgotten, but I don't, that you owe me nine thousand six hundred and fifty dollars, and that under Maryland law you can be jailed until it's paid." Then he must have said something mean, because she listened and then went on. "I don't care what proof you have, what proof you think you have. I'll move in just the same. And I suggest that you think this over: I'll be the plaintiff, you the defendant, when my suit comes to trial, and proof or no proof, though the plaintiff's lawyer takes a contingent fee, the defendant's has to be paid, in cash, before he goes to court. He wants a retainer, as it's called. So unless you want to shell out that retainer, you talk right when they call you today. But why must you talk at all? Ed, Mandy has treated you decently, not saying a word, not one, about the rotten reception you gave her, and I appeal to *your* decency now, before hitting you with a brick. But if you don't have any decency, Ed, I just happen to have a brick. That's all I wanted to say. Ed, did you hear me?"

When she hung up she was hysterical, and Mr. Wilmer, Steve, and I all had to take turns calming her. But at last she was quiet and said, "It wasn't myself I was thinking of, but of us, Ben, and our marriage. Because if he starts shooting his mouth off, even if not one word of it's true, I can't go home anymore. Oh, dear God, beat some sense in his head!"

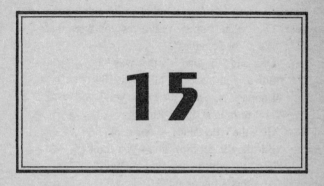

15

Mr. Wilmer begged me to stay with him and Mother there in the suite at the hotel, where they decided to spend the weekend, or part of the next week, until things would be settled in Baltimore. He said the suite could be enlarged by unlocking the door to a bedroom, and then I would be there with them. And I have to omit I was tempted to stay again in that hotel, with my own color TV and all, wearing Mother's nighties and having lunch in the coffee shop. But even more I wanted to be with Steve and thank him for what he had done, on account that at last I had a father who took up for me. So I drove home with him in his car, a Chevy, the way we had come over. On the way, we had dinner in a new place near Laurel, and I told him how I felt. I said, "It's so funny, here a week ago I was mad, at you and also at Mother, and sure that Vernick was the answer, that he would take me in. And now it's all come opposite. You're my father at last, and Mother's my mother at last, and Vernick's just a rat. How can that be?"

"Well, look at me. I was ready to jump off the roof. I mean I wanted to die, 'stead of which I drunk me some beer. Then when I opened my eyes you were there."

"It's all backwards."

"OK, and I'm glad it's that way."

"Steve, you mean it's all for the best?"

"I hope it is. We don't know yet."

"You're talking about Rick?"

"He's the wild deuce in our deck."

"But they'll get him, don't you think?"

"Yes, but will they get the money?"

"And that's important?"

"It's the whole story, Mandy."

"Anyhow, tomorrow should tell the tale."

"Or next week, looks like."

He said if Rick surrendered and still had most of the money, "maybe they decide he was forced and panicked afterward, and they let him up easy so he pleads guilty to some minor charge, like accessory, and gets a suspended sentence, something like that. With immunity for you, that ends it."

"Funny, when he ducked out on me, I hated him something awful. Now I don't. Now I feel sorry for him. It's all backwards."

"Mandy, life is like that."

I was looking forward, I guess, to another visit from him to me in my bed as I lay there and he would kiss me good night. But that wasn't to be for a while yet. We were no sooner home than the phone rang, and when he took it he said: "That was the *Washington Post*. They're sending a man out, and he'll have a photographer with him. So get yourself fixed up."

"Well? Isn't this all right?"

I motioned to the dress, and he said, "For me, perfect. Anything you put on always looks perfect to me, but if it's what you want, I don't know. That's all I meant. Don't change it for me."

"I bought a pantsuit in Baltimore."

"OK, put it on."

So I went upstairs and did, and as I came down he yelped to come quick, I was on TV. It was the evening news, and sure enough there I was, in a picture taken of me the summer before at the beach in a bikini which they dug up heaven knows where. And, brother, was I showing all I had. There was also a picture of Rick that didn't look like him, as it showed him wearing short hair, with a little grin on his face that gave him a queer expression. But what was said wasn't too bad, and in fact was halfway funny, as the announcer kidded the cops, the Baltimore police that is, for "the thorough and diligent way they've been following false leads." When it went off Steve kissed me, and I had trouble calming him down, as he was acting the least bit balmy.

Then the doorbell rang, and he let in the *Post* reporter, with the photographer he had. So he began putting questions to me, and I answered as well as I could, trying to small things down so nothing amounted to much. When Vernick was mentioned I just started to laugh and acted like it was all a joke. But it brought up the coat, and I had to get it out and pose for my picture in it, sitting and standing and walking around. So while that was going on, the doorbell rings again, and it's a guy from the *Baltimore Sun*, and he had a photographer too. So I had to do it all over again. Then the doorbell rings again, and it's a girl from the *Washington Star*, also with a photographer, to do a "feature" on me, though what a feature was I didn't know then and don't know now. So I do it again for her. And when we're just about finished up, the phone rings and it's for the man from the *Baltimore Sun*, with instructions to get dope on Mother's marriage. So I tell what I know about that, strictly sticking to it that she was so upset at me running off that way, that Mr. Wilmer wanted to make it up to her by having a wedding. I felt I did all right, and then at last they all went. Steve fixed us a couple of drinks, beer for him, Coke for me, and then we went to bed. Then, sure enough, here he came, being himself once more, to kiss me good night again and tell me that he loved me. So I kissed him and told him the same.

In the morning we got up real early, me still in my kimono, to grab the paper and see what it had about me. But it wasn't at all bad, except for what Rick's father, mother, and sister said about me, that I was a "Junior Jezebel" who had led a good boy astray "in a flagrantly immoral way." They said he'd led an exemplary life, not giving any trouble "until this girl came along." Why they'd put him out, why he had no home, that they didn't say, but the paper did, putting in about his arrests. Vernick was let out with a line: "No comment. Absolutely no comment at all" was all that he had to say and all that they put in. On page one were two pictures of me, one in the bikini, the other modeling the coat, but on the page that the story jumped to was a whole picture layout: Mother, in the green linen suit; Rick, the same shot as had been on TV; and me, more shots in the coat, another in the bikini, and one in a leotard, when I was twelve years old, from gym class in junior high, the cheese-cakiest one of all. And under it: JUNIOR JEZEBEL? Still and all, none of it was too bad.

I made coffee and toast for us, and while we ate on the breakfast room table, we read the paper, taking turns. Then Steve said get dressed, we were going to Baltimore to get there quick for whatever was in the works for me. So we rode over feeling close, but when we got to the hotel he didn't go up to the suite. He said he'd finish his breakfast and wait in the coffee shop. So when I went upstairs Mr. Wilmer looked kind of funny and said I'd better go in and see how my mother was doing. I knocked on the door of the bedroom, and when she told me come in I did and found her in bed, with papers all over the covers, not only the *Baltimore Sun* but the *Washington Post* and another Baltimore paper. And when she saw me she held out her arms and gathered me in and kissed me. She was in a beautiful black nightie, with a black bow in her hair and looking prettier than I'd ever seen her. She kissed me all over the face and back of the ears, and asked, "Have you seen them?" meaning the papers.

"I saw the *Post*. I thought it was pretty OK."

"OK? *OK?* It was perfect. That Ed Vernick, I shut him up! Did you see what he had to say?"

"He had nothing to say, just 'no comment.'"

"Keeping his head down from my brick!"

"You're just a sweet, crazy goof!"

So then she was laughing and Mr. Wilmer was there,

sitting on the bed, patting her. "The sun's coming up," he said.

"And I can go home again!"

"Mother? You mean, to *Hyattsville*?"

I omit I was somewhat surprised, because why she'd be going back there I didn't exactly see. But she said, "Home to me now is Lacuvidere, the place Ben took me to Thursday, when we got married—the house he built by his lake, up there in Frederick County, the house we *both* built by the lake, those beautiful golden days when Steve would be in New York and we could do things together. Mandy, he phoned one friend from Dover, telling the news, but that one friend was enough. When we got there and he carried me over the threshold, suddenly music started, and then there they all were with candles, his friends, bringing us into our home. For three hours they warmed us and cheered us and loved us. I couldn't have faced them again if Ed Vernick had shot off his mouth. That's what I mean, that 'I can go home again!'"

"Well, Mother, he didn't shoot it off."

"That's right, thanks to me."

She gave me a little hug, then jumped up and whipped off her nightie, so except for the bow in her hair, she had nothing on at all. She was simply beautiful. She opened the closet and took out a dress, a dark red one of grosgrained silk. But then she took out another, a dark blue with black binding on it at neck, sleeves, and hem. She said, "Mandy, I got it for you yesterday, after you left." Then she undressed me, so except for the ribbon in my hair, I was as naked as she was. We both stood in front of the mirror, she giving me kisses and slaps and slaps and kisses, a lot. And two funny things I noticed:

first, except in the face and hair, I was practically her twin in height, size, and shape, something I hadn't known. And second, Mr. Wilmer just sat there and smiled, making no move to go, and she let him. That seemed the funniest of all, when I thought about it later. I mean he didn't go and I didn't mind; I didn't know why. I didn't have a stitch on, and yet it seemed all right that he should be there looking on. Of course, not for long. I slipped into fresh underwear and the beautiful dress, feeling quite proud of myself at how I was going to look, going to sign my confession. When we were all dressed and breakfast was on the way up, she said, "Mandy, when this is all over, we'll have a surprise for you, one I think you're going to like. But first things first. Let's wind this awful thing up before we start something else."

We all three went down soon as we finished breakfast, said hello to Steve in the coffee shop, walked around to Mr. Clawson's, and then taxied to City Hall, where Mr. Haynes's office was. When we got there the same girl was there, the one who had worked the stenotype, as well as the tape recorder. Mr. Haynes brought us all in his private office and she handed him some papers, not yet stapled together, that seemed to be my confession. He read it, though pretty fast, as though he'd seen it before, and then gave it to me, saying, "Yes, Mandy, I think it's in order now. Will you sign it, here at the end, on the line she's marked with an X. Then initial each page."

But, like I told Mrs. Minot, curiosity killed the cat, and I wanted to read what I'd said. It was not what I'd said at all! It was all different and left out about the gun and how scared Rick and I were. It had in about the mink coat, but nothing about Rick backing out, or trying to, before being made at gunpoint. It was loused from beginning to end, and I yelped, "It's not what I said. It's been doctored!"

"Yes, Mandy? In what way doctored?"

Mr. Haynes was very cold, but I told him. More than I've put in here. By that time Mr. Clawson had had a look, and he chimed in too: "What's the big idea, Jack? Having Mandy's statement rewritten?"

"Well, we generally do. You have to pull it together so it makes some kind of sense."

"It made plenty of sense as she said it."

"Not to a jury it wouldn't."

"Since when is a jury so dumb?"

That was Mother, sounding like ground glass in a blender. By that time she'd had a look too, and she went on, "I've had to sit in court while cases were being tried, and my observation was not that juries were dumb, but that they weren't—that that was the trouble with them, from the lawyer's point of view. Could it be that you rewrote Mandy's statement as a way of convincing that boy?"

"I've said why I had it rewritten."

"You have indeed."

"You doubt my word?"

He was pretty ugly about it, but she said, "Come here."

He didn't move, and she went over to him. She leaned close, patted his cheek, and said, "You don't look like no lion tamer."

"Just like a lying son of a bitch?"

He laughed and she laughed, telling him, "You go wash your mouth out with soap! Why, the very idea, saying something like that in mixed company! And good-looking as you are, and truthful-looking! You stop cutting your eye at me, or I'll be falling for you! Where's the typescript? Of the tape? From the recording machine? She'll sign that, and that's all she'll sign, or we're starting all over again."

"Mr. Wilmer, you have a persuasive wife."

"Oh, she generally gets her way."

"And a damned beautiful wife."

"She'll pass in a crowd, no doubt."

"Pass in it? She'll light it up like a star shell."

By that time he had motioned to the girl, who got another paper out of her dispatch case, a thick one, all stapled up in a blue cover. Mother took it, glanced through it, flipping the pages over, and said, "OK, this is it. Mandy? Do you have a pen?"

So I signed, the girl stamped her notary seal on and signed, after having me raise my right hand and asking did I solemnly swear that the statement I had given here was the truth, the whole truth, and nothing but the truth. That seemed to be it. Mr. Haynes looked at Mother and said, "Mrs. Wilmer, since you are so very good-looking, and since your eyes do turn me to putty, I'll kick in with some very good news. It made the A.P. wire."

"What did? And what's the A.P. wire?"

"The story was sent out by the Associated Press. It hit them funny, the rude awakening you got on your wedding night."

"OK, but what's good about it?"

"It means that papers have it all over the country, so that boy will see it and, if he has any sense, surrender."

"Oh. Yes, I guess that would help."

"It'll be the end of this thing!"

"Or maybe not, Mr. Haynes."

"What makes you say that, Mandy?"

"He doesn't have any sense."

So then we all had lunch—Mr. Clawson, Mr. Haynes, Mr. Wilmer, Mother, and I—at Marconi's again, but I kept thinking of Steve, and when I mentioned him, Mr. Wilmer called the hotel, had him paged, and invited him. And he came. And Marconi's is a wonderful place, which did it big for Mr. Wilmer, and I loved the dishes they served but don't remember their names. So once again Mr. Wilmer begged me to stay and said we'd paint the town red, he, Mother, and I, "for a real Saturday night" and "when I say red I mean red. If there's one thing Baltimore has, it's bucketfuls of red paint." But Steve's face spoke to me, and I said I'd go back with him. Then, from the look on Mother's face, I knew she still had hopes that I would fall for him in more than a daughterly way. But Mr. Wilmer was frowning, not seeming to like it so much.

Anyhow, Steve and I drove home and hardly were in the house before things commenced to happen. First, of course, was the phone, and that was my first experience with the obscene call from some guy. You've no idea what they said, and you know you ought to hang up, and yet what you do is hang on from not believing what they'll say next. Then the doorbell, with people there you hadn't seen in a year, or thought of in all that time—beginning with Mrs. Minot, still nosing around for some dirt, asking if Mother got married and why I'm not held in jail. I told her, "Ask me no questions, I'll tell you no lies," and Steve told her, "You'll have to excuse us, please, we're awfully tired."

So I'd ask them in and talk a few minutes and Steve would shoo them out, saying, "We have to put in some calls" or "We have some friends coming in" or "We have to darn some socks" or whatever popped in his head. It went on all afternoon, and then at night we went out to the Bladensburg place for dinner. We got home around nine o'clock, and when the phone rang Steve took it. Then he handed me the receiver, saying, "Some guy calling you long-distance."

But he looked at me kind of queer, and when I answered I knew why. A boy's voice said, "Mandy Vernick, please."

"This is Mandy Vernick."

"Mandy, this is Rick."

"Oh! Well, hello and how are you, Rick?"

I tried to make it sound friendly, but he snarled when he said, "What's it to you how I am?"

"Rick, that's not very nice."

"Who says it's supposed to be nice?"

"OK. What do you want?"

"To tell you what you've got coming."

"What do you mean coming?"

"What do you think I mean? For what you've done to me, that's what I mean."

"Done to you? I did you a favor, that's what I did, putting them on your trail so you can be taken in before you do something else as silly as the last thing you did.

Rick, are you listening to me? If you give yourself up, right away, wherever you are, and turn that money in, they may not do much to you. I did everything I could to make it that you were forced at gunpoint against your will, and that's on my statement, *sworn*. But if you keep on being a jerk, that won't hold water at all, what I put in my statement. It'll be that you do want that money, that maybe *once* you were forced, but now you're hanging on all of your own free will. Rick, are you listening?"

"Bitch, are you?"

"Rick, that's no way to talk."

"OK. I'll knock off the talk and say what I mean to do. What I mean to do to you."

"And what's that?"

"Well, what do you think?"

"Listen, I don't go for riddles."

"Then, I'll make it plain. I'm killing you, Mandy. That's what I mean to do. You're going to wake up dead."

"And how can you kill me?"

"By shooting you through your lying, double-crossing, rotten little heart."

"Rick, will you listen to me?"

"No, Mandy, I don't have time."

Then came the dial tone and I knew he had hung up. Steve had been leaning close and said, "I heard it. That means we must call the cops."

16

So the next three hours were nice. I'll say they were, the kind of a nightmare you dream about all the rest of your life. After talking it over with me, holding my hand and telling me not to be scared, regardless of what Rick had said, Steve decided to call the Baltimore cops, not the Prince George's County cops or the Town of Hyattsville cops, though, of course, they were just down the street. So he did, first getting the number from information. He had to argue about it, first with one guy, then with another, till he finally got one who was actually in charge of the case. He was told to hold everything, to "keep the girl there in the house," and an officer would be over. Sure enough, the officer came, after a couple of hours, and heard us both tell our tale. But Steve's, it turned out, was just as important as mine. Because he was the one who heard it, what the girl had said, what the operator told Rick, before the connection was made:

"Deposit a dollar and a half, please." That told it, not much but a little, where the call had come from—at lease in a general way, Florida, California, Nevada, Arizona, or New Mexico. It wasn't much, but as the officer said, more than nothing. The main thing was Rick couldn't get there that night.

But that was just the beginning. Next off, the officer had to call Baltimore, "the Chief," as he called him, for orders on what to do next. So the Chief said take me in, to jail seemed to be the idea, "protective custody" so I wouldn't get shot. That's when Steve hit the roof, refusing to let me go for the reason I already was in custody, custody of my mother, and he was acting for her. Then he called Mr. Clawson, whose number he already had, and had him talk to the officer. The officer said orders were orders but that he would wait while Mr. Clawson called the Chief and the Chief called him back. So then we sat around and Steve put out some beer, when the officer kind of relaxed and wasn't so bullheaded to us. Then the Chief called and they talked, first the officer and then Steve. And Steve said, "Chief, who am I to tell you your business and how to run it? Just the same, it makes no sense, taking this girl in. In the first place it's wrong, and in the second place it's dumb. Because, look, suppose he calls again? Suppose he's stolen a car and is on his way to her? Or suppose he's traveling by bus? Or plane? Or however he's fixing to get here? And he puts in another call? Tonight? Tomorrow? Or tomorrow night? If she's here she can string it out, hold him on the line while the call is traced, which takes a few minutes, remember. If she's not here that does it, and nothing more can be done. If she is here we got a chance. And so far as him killing her goes, it won't happen, that I promise you. I have a gun, right here in this house, in the downstairs table drawer. I keep it under a permit. Have to; I drive a truck. So no one's going to shoot her."

The officer was leaning close, out there in the hall, to hear what was being said, and I could tell by how he was acting that Steve had put it across. It was a half hour before he left, as calls had to be made, to the Baltimore cops, the Hyattsville cops, and the Baltimore cops again, to set the stakeout up so we could catch Rick if he called, or at lease find out where he was. But at last he did leave, and then we could go to bed. So once more I wanted Steve there to tell me good night, and once more he came. He knelt by the bed, and I kissed him and at last told him about the island. He said, "But Mandy, you want an island, we'll have one, lessen they cost more than I think. Next month my rig will be paid for, and the house already is. We'll have money to buy one. And even now we can have clams. There's a place in Washington sells them, Little Necks, on the half shell!"

"Steve, now you're the goof."

"OK, but I love you."

"And thanks for tonight. What you did, I mean, saving me from going to jail."

"That was an idea, wasn't it?"

Next day was Sunday, and the papers didn't have it, but Steve said they're printed early and don't have the late stuff until Monday. Around ten Mother called, scared to death that I was in jail, and it turned out Mr. Clawson had called her the night before, but she wasn't in the hotel and got in too late to give him the callback he asked for. Of course, count on Mother; Saturday night, town-painting on Saturday night as long as the red held out was what she loved most of all. So when she was calmed down, I made breakfast for Steve and me, eating it in my kimono, which I shouldn't have done, as he could see plenty and once I caught him peeping. Then I dressed and the razzmatazz started—the same old thing, with people coming and Steve running them out, and the obscene bunch on the phone. So we started to go out for lunch, but a cop in a car stopped us and said we must stay in "to take any calls," as he put it, meaning calls from Rick. So we did, and some canned shrimp were there, which I fixed on toast, with some vegetable soup to start and ice cream to wind up, as Mother had always had some for me. For dinner I put out steaks to thaw and cooked them in the broiler, with a baked potato apiece, peas and onion, ice cream again for dessert, and salad to start. Steve was awful nice, paying me compliments on how good I cooked. At eight Rick called again, and Steve ducked out the front door to yell at the cop in his car that he should start the tracer going, calling in on his radio phone, so the phone company would get busy on it, as they had said they would. So I commenced doing my stuff, bawling and carrying on so Rick would enjoy himself, the scare he was giving me, and hang on to hear some more. And he did, for quite some time, but then all of a sudden hung up, before the tracer was run out all the way. But they did take it as far as St. Louis, which proved he was somewhere out West, as I had thought all along. Because it didn't look like, in Savannah, he would keep on with the trip that he and I had started. That more or less left the West. And this time

Steve heard the girl say, "Deposit one dollar, please," which seemed to mean he was closer, in El Paso or Denver or Omaha.

So we went to bed again, and I was happy and felt safe with Steve. Monday the papers had it, Rick saying he meant to kill me, but not a big story at all, or pictures or anything. Which seemed funny, but that's how it was. Then something had to be done to get some food in the house, as we were running low. So when Mrs. Minot came again to put her nose in it once more, right after Steve rang his replacement to take the truck to New York for still another trip, Steve got her into the act to go out and buy us some stuff. I made out a list for her and Steve gave her twenty dollars, so at last she said she would and went off in her car. Pretty soon she was back, with a shopping bag full of stuff and $6.42 in change, which Steve told her to keep "to help pay for your gas." So that relieved on the famine and also relieved on her. Because once she'd taken his money, she more or less had to shut up, the stuff she was talking around, as people had called in to tell me. It was kind of a gain all around.

That night the bell rang again, for the 1001st time, and when Steve opened the door it was Mother. "Seems so strange," she said, "to be ringing the bell of this house, instead of coming right in with my key."

So, of course, we said she could have and was more than welcome, but she said, "It's not my home anymore. I guess that's why I rang. My home, my new home, my real home, means so much to me, I can't let myself have two, even from force of habit."

She was dressed very quiet, for her, in a dark gray

dress, with a black crepe coat that she carried. And parked out front was the Caddy. But when I asked where Mr. Wilmer was, she said, "Paris. He flew over this morning on that business he had, which would have been waiting for him on our wedding trip. He sells liquor there, you know."

"But why didn't you go?" I asked. "I'd have been all right here in the house with Steve."

"Couldn't. Can't leave the country, you know."

"You mean on account of me?"

"The judge ruled it out."

"Then, Mr. Clawson called about it?"

"The answer was I had to stay here."

"Then I really loused you, Mother. I'm sorry."

"It's all right."

We all went in and sat down, and she did not throw it up to me, how the mess I'd got myself in was cutting her out of the trip. So then the bell rang again, and who was there was a girl, in jeans and T-shirt and loafers, a little bit older than I was, who waved at me from the hall and said, "Hello, Mandy. I'm Esther Childs," acting as though she knew me. I didn't place her at all but tried to act friendly with her, as I did with all the rest, and asked her into the living room, introducing her to Mother and Steve. We all sat down and she commenced talking along. She asked how I'd been. I said fine, and I asked how she'd been. She said fine. She said, "It's been a long time since Northwestern High."

"Well, not over a week."

"I graduated year before last."

"Yeah, I thought you looked older."

There may have been more, I don't know, but if it

wasn't making much sense, I didn't pay too much attention, as none of it did—the stuff that people got off after they got in the house. But all of a sudden Mother leaned toward her and said, like to warn her, "Watch it, Esther, please!" and pointed off to one side. When the girl's head snapped around, Mother grabbed her handbag. The girl started to scream, but Mother stepped out in the hall. When the girl followed, Steve grabbed her. Then Mother opened the bag and took out a gun, a shiny, snub-nosed thing with bullets showing. Said Mother, "Now, young lady, who are you, and what are you doing here?"

"Give me that gun! Give me..."

"Come on, say something!"

With that, Mother pointed the gun right at her and the girl started to scream, "No! No! No! Please!"

"Did you hear me?"

"Mrs. Wilmer, I'm Esther Davis."

"*Davis?* That's Rick's name."

"Yes, Ma'am. He's my brother."

I remembered then, Rick had mentioned a sister as the only one in his family who ever treated him decent. Mother went on, "He put you up to this?"

"Yes, Ma'am. He called."

"He sent you to kill Mandy?"

"Oh, no, Mrs. Wilmer. I couldn't have. He told me to get her bag, her handbag, to see if she still had the keys to the suitcase they bought in Baltimore to carry the money in."

"My God, Mandy! *Have* you?"

That was Steve and I couldn't answer, as it was the first I'd thought of the keys since we locked the money up in the suitcase that we bought in the Mondawmin

Center in Baltimore. My bag was there on the table, and at once I opened it up and dumped it in my chair so what was in it shook out—all kinds of different things, like a coin purse and Kleenex and ballpoint and lipstick and perfume. And, sure enough, here came the keys, two of them, flat ones, but little. Mother told Steve to take them, saying, "I think we must call Mr. Clawson, and, frankly, I don't know what to do next—with her, I mean."

"I *know* we have to call him."

So they did and, of course, spent a wonderful evening. Mother held Esther at gunpoint while the cops rang in and told us to wait, they'd be over. We did and they came after perhaps an hour, but when they got there they figured the gun was a local offense, a job for the Prince George's police. By that time Esther was begging to call her parents, so they let her and they came, the first I met Mr. Davis or Mrs. Davis, either one. Mother let them in, and they no sooner laid eyes on Esther than they commenced bawling her out. I said, "If you'd been nicer to Rick, 'stead of bawling him out all the time, same as you're bawling her out, it all might have turned out different. Junior Jezebel talking, if you don't like it, who cares if you do or not?"

"Jezebel, cool it! Father talking!"

That was Steve, and everyone laughed, even Esther.

Next off, Steve, Mother, and I were down in the county police station, at the building they have in Hyattsville, to sign on for the charge against Esther. By that time the papers had it, and the reporters were there with photographers, and Steve gave out for them. They took Mother's picture, and the cops let her hold the gun, which she did, looking like one of those gunmen's molls in a movie. Then we all went to the Cucaracha, a place in Cottage City where there was kind of a show with jokes, but they only had one joke, which was the girl scratching herself, like bit by the *cucaracha*. Then Mother kicked in, to her and her dancing partner, and they did the hat dance for her. So she was living once more, laughing and having fun. When she drove us home in the Caddy, she was weeping as we got out, Steve and I. She said, "I hate to go. I wish I could spend the night."

"Well, what's stopping you?" asked Steve.

"I can't. I have to get back to the hotel."

"You're still there?"

"Yes, will be till Ben gets back."

Then at last, Steve asked what I wanted to ask, but for some reason hadn't, "How did you know she had that gun?"

"The funny way she was acting, the goofy way she talked. What was she doing there? What did she want? It seemed to me she was hugging the bag too close, so I decided to have me a look."

"I'll say you did."

"Mother, I never once thought of it."

"You love someone, you think."

She kissed me and kissed Steve, and then he and I got out. She drove off, looking beautiful as she waved to us.

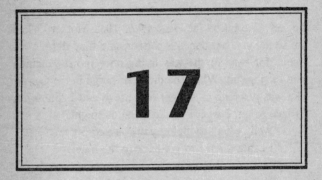

17

Next day was more of the same, until maybe four o'clock, when an officer rang the bell, a detective in regular clothes, from the Baltimore department. He said his name was O'Brien and was kind of a good-looking guy, friendly and pleasant and nice, except he said he must "take me out." I said, "Take me in; is that what you mean?"

"No just out, not in."

"What's the difference, if I may ask?"

"Out means I just ride you around, to get you away from this house. In would mean in to jail."

"Like in protective custody?"

"Something like that, yes."

But Steve was there and got in it, of course. He asked, "What's the idea? Why?"

"Rick Davis is why. He's back."

"Oh? How do you know?"

"They found his car."

"Car? He didn't have any car."

"Now he has, one that he stole or that somebody stole, with California plates. They found it down the street, on the old Hot Shoppe parking lot."

"How did they know it was his?"

Until then he'd been pleasantly shifty, like to tell no more than he had to. But now he seemed to change his mind. After studying Steve he said, "OK, hold on to your hat."

"I'm holding it. Shoot."

"By the money that was in it."

"You mean they got it back?"

"All of it except, of course, the five grand they knew about that Mandy found on the floor of the getaway car when they switched and split up with Rick at Mondawmin Center."

"How much actually?"

"Hundred and fifteen grand."

"Then, I was of real help, wasn't I?"

"I'll say it was real, Mandy, plenty."

By now he was enjoying the sensation he'd caused and really wanted to talk. He went on to explain "how the job was done right here by the Hyattsville police, after they called us about it." He said, "Even if he was watching, which they think he was not, he'd hardly have known his car was being worked on." He told how they got their locksmith, the one near the county building, to come and bring his depth gauge, whatever that was, to take a reading with it of the car, of the lock on the trunk of the car, then go back to his shop real quick and file a key. Once they had that they opened the trunk, and, sure enough, there was the suitcase which they opened with the keys I had turned in. Soon as they had the money, they put phone books in the suitcase, locked it up like it had been, and then locked the trunk, so everything was just as it had been when he came back to the car. Then they posted their stakeout to wait until he would come.

But Steve wasn't done with him yet. He went to the table drawer and took out his gun, a blue one, pretty big, and showed it to him. Then he got out two papers in envelopes, one his permit to carry it, the other his certificate, from the Silver Spring Small Arms Range, of how good he could shoot. He said, "OK, Mr. O'Brien, look them over. There's a gun good as yours, and there's my certificate that says I shoot good as you do. Then, why can't I protect her? Why must you take her away?"

"This girl means a lot to you?"

"She means everything to me. I love her. I'm practically a father to her."

"Then, get with it. Her life is in danger. I don't care how good you shoot; she could be killed, before you could draw, before you could even take aim, by a shot through the window, or some other cockeyed way. But if she's not here . . . !"

"I got it now. OK."

"The stakeouts are on everywhere, outside this house, outside his parents' house, around the car. And the dragnet's on too, with two officers going around with kids who know him by sight, to lunchrooms, stores, and bars. We'll get him, but until we do, let's watch out for *her*."

"I said OK. So OK."

"Then, OK."

"How long is this going to take?"

"Till we get him."

"That could go on quite a while."

"Not like the grass on her grave."

"How about dinner?"

"Let's cross that bridge when we come to it. It's not dinner time yet."

Steve looked at me, then took out his wallet and slipped me a twenty-dollar bill. He said, "When dinner time comes, ask Mr. O'Brien if he'll have dinner on me." He thought, then slipped me ten dollars more. "And 'stead of riding around, a picture show might be better. If you invite him he might accept."

"OK, Steve, I will."

I kissed him and whispered, "I love you," the last words on this earth I ever said to him, and I'm glad they were the ones, the last ones he heard from me.

We got in Mr. O'Brien's car, which had no police markings on it, and commenced driving around. But that wasn't too much fun, so I remembered what Steve had said and asked would he like to see a movie, "as Steve's guest, my foster father." So he said OK, and I figured out he had no way to charge it up as expense and at the same time didn't care to spend his own money on a girl who meant nothing to him. Then we parked and walked to the Riverdale Plaza, and the picture was *Fool's Parade*. But we didn't like it much and walked out, when from the booth in the lobby I called Steve to find out how things stood. But who answered was Mother, as she'd driven over again, like the day before, to keep company and help out marking time. And she was all excited I'd called, telling me stay away, that the officers felt my life was in danger, so I mustn't attempt to come home until Rick was caught. That I already knew, but I thanked her and asked when Mr. Wilmer would get home. She said he was flying back next day, "when I hope this whole thing will be over, and we can relax and be happy."

"You heard about the money?"

"Oh my, and was that a relief. Because to get immunity for you, he had to pledge to make good the whole shortage, the heist as everyone calls it. And, Darling, he's very well off, but a hundred and twenty thousand would have been a terrible blow, even to him. But five thousand isn't so bad."

"Have you told him?"

"Oh, yes, I called him at once."

She asked where she could reach me, and I said, "You can't. I'll be moving around with the officer. I'm in a theater now, calling from the lobby, and where we go next I don't know. But I'll keep in touch. I'll be calling you."

"OK, but not before nine. I'd say around ten would be better. Steve has asked me to dinner, and he's been so nice in this thing, to you and Ben and me, that I want to act friendly to him. And besides, by ten it could all be over. The police think Rick will wait until dark and then make his move against you, or try to."

"OK. Animal, vegetable, or mineral?"

"*What* did you say, Mandy?"

"The surprise—can't you give me a hint?"

"Oh, Darling, don't spoil it for Ben. It means so much to him. I promise you it'll be big, and I think you're going to like it."

"Then, OK."

"At ten? You'll call?"

"Yes, Mother. I love you."

And those were the last words I said to her, God rest her pretty, sweet soul.

It said in the afternoon papers that Esther was out on $1,000 bail, and I called her, after looking the Davises up, fortunately remembering their name, John P., from the piece that came out in the paper. I wanted to tell her I had no hard feelings, that I understood she'd been put, made to do what she did by Rick. But once again I was calling one person and another came on the line. It was a boy's voice kind of muffled, the way people speak when they don't want to say who they are. But all of a sudden I knew who it was. I said, "Rick, what are you doing there?"

Then he commenced cussing me out, saying awful things to me, so filthy and mean and obscene I can't write them down. I couldn't make myself. I said, "Rick, you stop talking like that! Stop saying such things to me."

"Listen, bitch, saying's just the beginning. The rest of it's what I do! I'm going to get you if it's the last thing I do on this earth! Do you hear me? Are you listening?"

"Rick, *you* listen to *me*! You give yourself up, do you hear? Or someone's going to get you in a way you don't expect!"

Those were the last words I said to him, and I hope he remembered them when he died that night on our lawn.

* * *

He hung up on me, and, of course, I told Mr. O'Brien. He went into action fast, calling the Hyattsville police, not waiting to go out to the car and use his radio phone but doing it right there in the theater, to tip them that Rick was home. So they closed in in a couple of minutes, but Rick gave them the slip. And how he gave them the slip, it turned out later, was to put his mother's dress on, run a ribbon through his hair, and walk out of the house, right in front of their eyes. He was wearing shorts, and with the dress down to his knees they didn't show at all. So with that long hair of his and the sissy walk that he had, no one suspicioned him. That sissy walk, if you ask me, was part of the trouble with him. And all that took plenty of time, what with Mr. O'Brien standing by, there in the theater lobby, after giving the number in of the pay station there for the callback he asked them for. It was going on eight when he finally got word that they didn't have Rick, so at last we could go to the car and think about dinner. So I suggested the Bladensburg place and we went there, and I found out about an officer, that he doesn't stint himself when it's at somebody else's expense. He had shrimp salad to start, then steak, baked potato, salad, and pie a la mode to wind up. So I had the same, and the check was $15.75. I left a $4.25 tip, and we went out and got in the car.

We crossed the bridge and drove past the house. At the corner a flashlight came on and waved, and Mr. O'Brien stopped. An officer, one in uniform, stepped to the window and whispered a while. Then Mr. O'Brien drove on, first taking a right to turn the corner. "I'm circling the block," he said. "They want me to park out front, so if we're needed we'll be on call."

"If *I'm* needed, you mean?"

"Something like that, I would say."

"Why don't you rig up a bullhorn? Set it up so I can talk into it? If Rick's here he'll know where I am, that he hasn't a chance to get me and will perhaps listen to me."

"It's an idea, at that. I'll call it in."

He took three more rights, then pulled in to the curb a few steps down from the house. It was dark, with the front light not yet on, as, of course, it had been broad daylight when Mother and Steve went out. He commenced talking into his radio phone, unhooking the receiver from the dashboard and pressing buttons and stuff. Then he hung his receiver up, or mike, or whatever it's called, and said, "They're sending the bullhorn over, be here in a couple of minutes. Now, what are you going to say?"

"Well, I don't know. I hadn't thought."

"I want to hear it."

"You mean now?"

"That's it."

"Can't I just start to talk and act natural?"

"And louse it? No."

"Well, what do you want me to do?"

"Pretend I'm him. Talk to me."

So I commenced with the pretending, getting off stuff like, "Rick, this is Mandy. Rick, are you there, do you hear me? Rick, they have the money, they found the car, and there's no use you holding out. Rick, they're going to get you, so why not give yourself up now?" Stuff like that, but then Mr. O'Brien cut in, "What are you scared of? What's bugging you?"

"Who says I'm scared of anything?"

"Well, your mouth's trembling."

"My mouth always trembles when I have to say something by heart. And who says I should learn it by heart? Listen, Mr. O'Brien, suppose you attend to the copping, while I do the talking my own self, and in my own way; you don't mind? I'll make it plain, don't worry."

"Then, OK."

There may have been more, I don't know. We jawed at each other quite some little time. But during while it went on, a car passed up the street, stopped up near the corner, and backed into the curb. Then it pulled ahead, and backed up again, to park. As the lights went out, a man and a woman got out and started walking toward us. They had come some little ways before I realized they were Mother and Steve. They started toward the house but then stopped and turned back, as though hearing somebody speak. Steve stepped to the curb, where a car was parked, and I heard him say, "OK." Then the two of them started back, to the car, not to the house. She took Steve's arm real friendly, and it crossed my mind how pretty she looked from behind, just walking along. It crossed my mind to wonder if I was as pretty as that, as she sometimes said I was. Then I was screaming all of a sudden, without even knowing why. And then I did know why—it was to warn her, but I was too late. A shadow had moved out from the cedar tree, the one on the left-hand side of the walk. Then it moved fast, as though to cut her off. Then it darted, and I heard Rick speak my name. By that time she had stopped, and Steve had stepped in between. Then fire cut the night, from the shadow, and Steve went down. Then fire cut the night again, and Mother went down. Then fire cut the night from all sides, and Rick went down.

Then I was running up the sidewalk, not knowing how I got there, or how I'd got out of the car. Hands reached out to grab me, but I shook loose and went running on. Then, by the flashlights the police were holding, there was my darling mother, dead. And there was Steve, his drawn gun still in his hand. And there was Rick, still in his mother's dress, the red ribbon still in his hair.

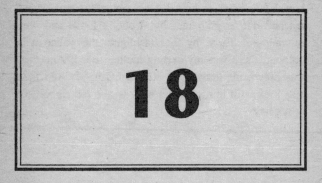

18

Then I was on the sidewalk beside Mother, sitting there holding her hand, while the officers went around making notes and taking flashlight pictures. Then a guy was there, asking who called for a bullhorn. "I did," said Mr. O'Brien, appearing from somewhere, "but it won't be needed now. Take it back." I began kissing Mother's hand, and then began kissing *her*, on the mouth, I mean, but it was so cold I was terrified and started to wail. I wailed louder and louder and louder, like some kind of a banshee, and heard Mr. O'Brien say, "This girl is in pretty bad shape, and I'm taking her to Prince George's General." But I kept right on wailing while he stretched me out on my back and tried to get me quiet. Not that he did, at all. Then an ambulance was there, and two guys lifted me onto a stretcher and tucked a blanket around me. Then I was inside the ambulance, and then in some kind of a room with women and kids and guys with bandaged heads—the accident ward, I guess. But Mr. O'Brien was there and got action on me pretty quick. An intern bent over me, where I was still on the stretcher, and then had me carried away by orderlies in green smocks.

Then I was in bed, in a room, with my clothes all taken off, and he was jabbing me in the backside with a needle. Then he said to Mr. O'Brien, "That ought to do it for a while."

Next thing I knew, I was lying under a sheet, with a hospital gown on that barely came to my waist, and I was sobbing into my hands, which I was holding over my eyes. And I heard some woman say, "That girl in the other bed is driving me insane. All she does is whoop and holler and bawl. I can't read, I can't sew, I can't sleep, I can't think!" Then another woman said, "It's OK, I've arranged to move you out, into another room. *Now!*" When I looked a nurse was there, helping a woman get up from the other bed, put her kimono on, and leave. I was alone for a minute, but the crying kept right on. Then another nurse came in, carrying a bottle, and she threw back the sheet and took off my hospital gown, so I was naked. She said, "Now you have the room to yourself, and I'm going to give you a massage—that ought to quiet you down. But if it doesn't, if you still can't get control, then I have to slap you. Do you hear?"

"Yes, Miss, I hear."

"Not as punishment. It's the indicated treatment."

"I'll do my best, I'll try."

"You can if you make yourself."

So she started the massage, slobbing the lotion on,

which was what she had in the bottle, witch hazel I think. And I tried to hold in, but pretty soon the sobs broke out once more. Then *pow*, here came the slap, and then another and another. But I didn't like it too much and started to scream. She slapped me still harder, but then suddenly she stopped. Then I heard a man's voice say, "Perhaps if you leave me with her, I can get her quiet. It's all right, I'm her father."

When I twisted around to see, she was leaving and Mr. Wilmer was there. "What do you mean you're my father?" I yelled at him. "You're nothing but my stepfather, the guy that married my mother . . . *and she's dead*!"

I really came out with it, but he took me under the arms, the way you take a child, lifted me up, and carried me to a chair, where he sat down with me in his lap. Then he reached for the sheet and pulled it over me, for warmness, but the part next to him was naked. Then he whispered, "If you want to cry, little Mandy, OK, let it come, nobody's going to slap you. But don't be surprised if I start crying too. I've had about all I can take, and I loved her too, you know."

"When did you get back?"

"This morning."

"What time is it now?"

"Just after two o'clock."

"And what day is it?"

"Wednesday."

"Then, it was last night that it happened?"

"That's right. I was so glad, coming off the plane, that I'd be seeing her soon, *and* you, and then I was paged at the airport. When I went to the office, Clawson's wire was waiting for me."

Suddenly I realized I wasn't crying anymore, and asked, "Why did you say you're my father?"

"Mandy, I am."

"We fixed it that Steve was my father."

"I know about that. But I am."

"I asked you why you say so."

"It started when I was eighteen, gassing up in a filling station, when a girl ran in off the street, a teenage girl in slacks, to get a Coke from the machine. I couldn't take my eyes off her, and as she started out I said, 'Hey.'

"'Well, hey your own self,' she answered.

"'Where you think you're going?'

"'Well, it's Saturday, isn't it?'

"'And what does that have to do with it?'

"'On Saturday you wouldn't know *where* you're going.'

"'Then, that means you're coming with me?'

"By that time she was at the door of the car looking me over and held the Coke bottle at me for me to take a swig. About that time the guy came with my change, and she helped herself to a dime. She put in a call, then came and got in beside me. She said, 'I told Mother I'd run into friends, and she gave me till six o'clock.' I swore to have her back on time and ran her down to our beach house, one that my family had on the Bay, between the bridge and Annapolis Harbor. But it was late September, and we had it all to ourselves, the happiest day of my life—completely silly and mad, with that mad, wonderful girl. We went swimming, she in my mother's bikini, I in my own trunks, and then we came back to the beach house. I got her home at six sharp, and her mother came out to shake hands and congratulate her on having 'punctual, dependable friends.'"

"OK, and what happened then?"

"I had to go off to college. Yale."

"Well? And what happened then?"

"Mandy, you know, don't you?"

"Steve told me a little."

"Then there's no need for me to say more. I was stunned when she married Vernick. But, say this for her: she'd been going with him and honestly thought he was the one."

"And when did you find out that you were?"

"The second I laid eyes on you."

"Last week, you mean?"

"You're the image of my little sister, whom your mother never knew, as she died before that day at the beach. And that same day I proved it by watching your lips, how they trembled, like hers used to do, when I made you recite that day. Remember? 'The Rime of the Ancient Mariner'? You looked like a cute little bunny, a rabbit eating lettuce. That night I convinced your mother, and we were going to tell you as soon as that mess was over."

"Is that the surprise you had?"

"Yes, of course."

"I went nuts trying to guess."

"Mandy, you also look like your mother, and that's what cost her her life. That boy mistook her for you. She died that you might live."

"It's what makes it so hard for me."

He held me close, and I knew, of course, it was true, that I'd found my father at last, and was glad, but not very much. Actually, I didn't feel anything, perhaps on account of what I'd been through. He began talking some more, about Steve, and the "glory-hole scapula he wore around his neck, a card with that title, which directed that he be cremated if he got killed in a crash and his ashes scattered on Number One. So his family are doing that." And he also mentioned Rick, "whose family claimed his body and are burying him in the plot that they have in one of the cemeteries. I don't know which one and really don't much care." I said I didn't either and to please not talk about it. But he said, "I'm leading to something, Mandy: *her* I want near us, where we'll be living now—at the house on the lake, *our* home, the one I had with her, that she helped build and lived in just one night. I want to bury her on our island."

"Your . . . *what* did you say?"

"We had an island, she and I."

"I want to hear about it!"

I popped out with that pretty loud, and pulled away from him so the sheet slid off and I was naked again. He looked at me very strange but got the sheet from the floor, put it over me again, and went on, "When the water was analyzed, of Dickinson's Run on my place, it was right for fermenting grain, but to pump it I had to dam up the stream. So, of course, that made a lake, but when the water rose an island was made out there, a beautiful green knoll, full of laurel and pine and oak, just out from the shore. They opened the sluiceway at sunrise, and by noon when we got there, your mother and I in the car, with the picnic lunch she had made, the island was already formed, with the lake rising fast. We sat there talking about it, how it would be our place, our love nest that we would have, where we'd hold hands and be happy. I said, 'We're starting tomorrow, soon as the bridge is put in. The lumber is being delivered today, construction will take no more than two hours, and then romance can begin. It won't be anything fancy, just a footbridge two boards wide. But it'll have a handrail on it, in case the lady gets stewed.'" He explained, "That was a gag we had, that occasionally she got stewed. She didn't, but she liked a glass of champagne."

"Two glasses, Mr. Wilmer."

"So OK, she liked a whole bottle!"

"And then had to go wee-wee."

On that we both burst out crying, holding each other close. Then, like with her that day, I could taste the salt of his tears. I said, "Go on about the island. Are we going to go there too? Is it going to be our island?"

"Don't you want to be near her, Mandy?"

"Oh yes! And near you, too."

"So we were kidding alone when trouble appeared or what looked like trouble to her. Five deer—a stag, three does, and a fawn—stepped out of the brush over there, walked to the edge of a lake they'd never seen before, and started looking unhappy. And *she* started looking unhappy. I said, 'Hey! Quit screwing your face up like that! And besides, what are they glawming about? In the first place, there's plenty to eat over there, laurel and dogwood and grass, and plenty of water to drink. In the second place, the bridge will be built tomorrow, and if it's good enough for you it's good enough for them— and they don't even drink champagne!' And more of the same. She said, 'Well, I haven't said anything?' Unfortunately, Mandy, she could talk louder saying nothing than anyone else can whooping. And then, anticlimax, here came the deer, swimming. Or at least four of them did, the stag and the three does. But the fawn was afraid and hung back. So, of course, his mother had to go back. The three others paid no attention, but when they reached our side they went on to the salt lick that was down the hill from us. But on the far bank it kind of tore your heart, the doe's efforts to lead Junior in, and his fear of the water. I chimed in with more of the same, 'No reason, no reason at all, that he can't stay right where he is. Tomorrow he'll cross in style.'

"And then, Mandy, disaster struck.

"On our side, a dog appeared on the shore, just a cur, just a wild dog. They're a feature you don't think much about, but they're murder just the same to all wild things in the woods. He didn't bark, a very bad sign, just pricked up his ears and plunged in. It took him no more than half a minute to swim those twenty yards, but when he walked out and shook himself, Mama was waiting for him. A deer's no match for a dog, and all she could do was strike at him with her front hooves, but he had to deal with her before he could kill the fawn, which he at once proceeded to do, charging at her, growling, and snapping. So then he got a surprise. Do you know what it was, Mandy?"

"Mother, I would say."

"That's right, Mandy, you guessed it. That dog had hardly showed when she was out of the car, scrambling down the hill to the water's edge. She whipped off her dress, hit the drink, came out, and faced the dog. He tore in, growling and snapping at her legs, but she grabbed him back of the ears, mashed his head to the ground, and then got hold of his tail. Mandy, she swung him like some kind of a hammer, like in the hammer throw of some non-Olympic games! One, two, three, around and around and around, and then she let him go. So he was yipping up in the air as he sailed over the lake, but she didn't even wait to hear him splash. She grabbed that little fawn, and with Mama pushing alongside, trotting, splashing, and swimming, she brought him across to our side, where he went trotting off to have his turn at the salt lick. *She didn't know what fear was!*"

At that, he burst out crying again, and I did. He said, "Mandy, she loved jokes and music and dancing. Pleasure people are brave people! Laughing *is* brave!"

"Don't hold back, let it come!" I told him in between sobs. "I love you. Now I know you're my father. Now I do!"

I kissed him then, on the mouth, holding him close so he would know I was his. When our crying had kind of died off, he said he would go to court and acknowledge me so I could use his name, which he did and I did. So now I'm Amanda Wilmer, five foot two, 36-24-35, of Lacuvidere, Rocky Ridge, Maryland. It was at Lacuvidere, a beautiful, beautiful place, a one-story white house overlooking the lake, with a veranda like at Mount Vernon, that they held the first service for her. Then the bearers carried her down and across, holding her high on the bridge so they could go single file. I almost died when I heard "Dust to dust," and the minister crumbled earth on the coffin. But then my father touched me, and he was crying too but looking in a direction he wanted me to look, and when I did, there was a little fawn, another little fawn, a tiny spotted thing that couldn't have been more than one day old, lying under a tree, holding still so as not to be seen. And I knew what was in his mind: that in the little creature a new life was starting out, and it seemed a beautiful thing that it should be staring at her as they lowered her into the grave.

That's all. I've told it.

MORE MYSTERIOUS PLEASURES

PETER O'DONNELL
MODESTY BLAISE
Modesty and Willie Garvin must protect a shipment of diamonds from a gentleman about to murder his lover and an *un*civilized, sheik.   #216 $3.95

SABRE TOOTH
Modesty faces Willie's apparent betrayal and a modern-day Genghis Khan who wants her for his mercenary army.   #217 $3.95

A TASTE FOR DEATH
Modesty and Willie are pitted against a giant enemy in the Sahara, where their only hope of escape is a blind girl whose time is running out.   #218 $3.95

I, LUCIFER
Some people carry a nickname too far . . . like the maniac calling himself Lucifer. He's targeted 120 souls, and Modesty and Willie find they have a personal stake in stopping him.   #219 $3.95

THE IMPOSSIBLE VIRGIN
Modesty fights for her soul when she and Willie attempt to rescue an albino girl from the evil Brunel, who lusts after the secret power of an idol called the Impossible Virgin.   #220 $3.95

ELIZABETH PETERS
CROCODILE ON THE SANDBANK
Amelia Peabody's trip to Egypt brings her face to face with an ancient mystery. With the help of Radcliffe Emerson, she uncovers a tomb and the solution to a deadly threat.   #209 $3.95

THE CURSE OF THE PHAROAHS
Amelia and Radcliffe Emerson head for Egypt to excavate a cursed tomb but must confront the burial ground's evil history before it claims them both.   #210 $3.95

DELL SHANNON

CASE PENDING
In the first novel in the best-selling series, Lt. Luis Mendoza must solve a series of horrifying Los Angeles mutilation murders.   #211 $3.95

ACE OF SPADES
When the police find an overdosed junkie, they're ready to write off the case—until the autopsy reveals that this junkie *wasn't* a junkie.   #212 $3.95

EXTRA KILL
In "The Temple of Mystic Truth," Mendoza discovers idol worship, pornography, murder, and the clue to the death of a Los Angeles patrolman.   #213 $3.95

KNAVE OF HEARTS
Mendoza must clear the name of the L.A.P.D. when it's discovered that an innocent man has been executed and the real killer is still on the loose.   #214 $3.95

DEATH OF A BUSYBODY
When the West Coast's most industrious gossip and meddler turns up dead in a freight yard, Mendoza must work without clues to find the killer of a woman who had offended nearly everyone in Los Angeles.   #315 $3.95

DOUBLE BLUFF
Mendoza goes against the evidence to dissect what looks like an air-tight case against suspected wife-killer Francis Ingram—a man the lieutenant insists is too nice to be a murderer.   #316 $3.95

JOE GORES

A TIME OF PREDATORS
When Paula Halstead kills herself after witnessing a horrid crime, her husband vows to avenge her death. Winner of the Edgar Allan Poe Award.   #215 $3.95

NAT HENTOFF

BLUES FOR CHARLIE DARWIN
Gritty, colorful Greenwich Village sets the scene for Noah Green and Sam MacKibbon, two street-wise New York cops who are as at home in the Village's jazz clubs as they are at a homicide scene.   #208 $3.95

WILLIAM DeANDREA

THE LUNATIC FRINGE
Police Commissioner Teddy Roosevelt and Officer Dennis Muldoon comb 1896 New York for a missing exotic dancer who holds the key to the murder of a prominent political cartoonist.   #306 $3.95

BRIAN GARFIELD
DEATH WISH
Paul Benjamin is a modern-day New York vigilante, stalking the rapist-killers who victimized his wife and daughter. The basis for the Charles Bronson movie.   #301 $3.95

DEATH SENTENCE
A riveting sequel to DEATH WISH. The action moves to Chicago as Paul Benjamin continues his heroic (or is it psychotic?) mission to make city streets safe.   #302 $3.95

TRIPWIRE
A crime novel set in the American West of the late 1800s. Boag, a black outlaw, seeks revenge on the white cohorts who crossed him and left him for dead. "One of the most compelling characters in recent fiction"—Robert Ludlum.   #303 $3.95

FEAR IN A HANDFUL OF DUST
Four psychiatrists, three men and a woman, struggle across the blazing Arizona desert—pursued by a fanatic killer they themselves have judged insane. "Unique and disturbing"—Alfred Coppel.   #304 $3.95